Charles Fort
Never Mentioned
Wombats

Also by Gene DeWeese & Robert Coulson:

NOW YOU SEE IT/HIM/THEM . . .
a Joe Karns adventure

Charles Fort
Never Mentioned
Wombats

GENE DEWEESE & ROBERT COULSON

Introduction by

WILSON TUCKER

DOUBLEDAY & COMPANY, INC.
GARDEN CITY, NEW YORK 1977

All of the characters in the book
are fictitious, and any resemblance
to actual persons, living or dead,
is purely coincidental.

Library of Congress Cataloging in Publication Data

DeWeese, Gene.
Charles Fort never mentioned wombats.

I. Coulson, Robert, joint author. II. Title.
PZ4.D5155Ch [PS3354.E929] 813'.5'4
ISBN: 0-385-12111-3
Library of Congress Catalog Card Number 76–23756

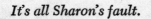

It's all Sharon's fault.

Contents

The Bamboo Mite Gap—An Introduction
by Wilson Tucker   ix

I.   "Charles Fort Never Mentioned Wombats"   1

II.   "We Don't Have *Everything* Figured
       Out Yet!"   7

III.   "What Did He Do, Unravel a Brillo Pad?"   19

IV.   "That Clown Must've Taken Lessons in
       Hokey Dying"   30

V.   "An Abominable Pedestrian, Maybe?"   37

VI.   "You Couldn't Fool Blind Freddy with a
       Line Like That"   44

VII.   "They Looked at Me Like I Was a Ratbag"   64

VIII. "I'm in No Shape to Save the World Tonight"   80

IX.   "I'd Never Have Made It on Social Security"   89

X.   "Why Should We Believe a Wishy-washy
       Disk That Talks Funny?"   107

XI.   "Hello? Is Anyone There?"   114

XII.   "Temporarily Can We Malfunctions Cause"   119

XIII. "You Make Me Sound Like the Hero's Dog!"   128

XIV.   "I Don't Think I'm Going to Buy *This*
       Gag Either!"   139

XV.   "Take a Deep Breath and Hold Perfectly Still"   146

XVI.   "You're Not a Porovian?"   153

XVII. "*Maurtiss, This Is Simply Too Much!*"   160

XVIII. "Don't You Believe *Anything* Is Real?"   166

XIX.   "They Shoulda' Quit While They Were
       Ahead"   169

XX.   "All I Promise Is a Half-baked Theory"   170

The Bamboo Mite Gap—An Introduction

I asked the man in the seat just ahead of me if he had ever seen a wombat. I got the strangest look in return, a stare that was almost a glare, and then came the grudging admission that he *had* seen one—just once. The answer seemed rather evasive, or suspicious.

And that was how I met Joe Karns.

As I got to know him better on that long flight, I mentally classified him as a mild-mannered reporter. I'd heard or read that description in my youth, and now the phrase fitted him. He was not rowdy or boisterous, as were many of his fellow travelers, and he didn't open up to a stranger as quickly as the others. *They* were a talkative lot, but their conversations made little sense to someone not in their circle—just as the jargon of my profession would make small sense to an outsider. Joe Karns was the quiet, solid type of citizen who was friendly enough once you got to know him, but he wouldn't make the overtures.

We were flying from Los Angeles to Sydney, New South Wales, on a twenty-hour Air New Zealand flight.

I had made that tedious trip a few times before and usually slept the hours away; the night-time movies offered in flight seldom interested me, the reading matter tended to be too many weeks or months old, and the one or two really curvilinear stewardesses working the Honolulu to Auckland leg of the flight would put up with just so much staring before they retired to the otherwise empty first-class cabin for privacy. But there was precious little sleep *this* trip. The companions of Joe Karns saw to that.

Those companions were "fans," they said.

Through Joe, and later some of the others, I learned that sixty of them were flying to Australia to attend a science fiction convention in Melbourne. None of them had visited Australia before, but some of them actually believed that kangaroos could—and would—leap from downtown alleys to mug them—relieve them of their cash. Others were of the opinion that native animals such as koalas and wombats could be found wandering the streets of the quieter suburbs, and could be picked up and brought home again as house pets. One fellow asked if it were true that human blood tended to lodge in the head because the people down under walked and lived upside down, in contrast to dwellers in the Northern Hemisphere.

These were Joe's science fiction "fans."

I found their jargon interesting, even fascinating, but not always comprehensible. Several of them took turns at a typewriter, typing on mimeograph stencils rather than paper, and one participant said they were engaged in "banging out a one-shot." One poor stewardess was as confused as I was when they asked for an "enchanted duper" on which to print those stencils, and the fans were disappointed when she finally understood them and had to tell them there was no mimeograph on board. It was finally made clear that a "one-shot" was a mimeographed pamphlet, but I never learned why a duplicator should be enchanted.

One of the anecdotes they told to help keep me awake—and they weren't talking to me, but to each other across the aisles—concerned a fan who had a reputation as a rounder, a ladies' man. I gathered that this fellow always carried with him a supply of calling cards which, instead of announcing his business affiliation, bluntly said he was a stud and that the lady who received the card was welcome to make an appointment for his services. The anecdote described his comeuppance.

When he attended a science fiction convention in Bellefontaine, Ohio, a few years ago, some of the gagsters in that city prepared his motel room in advance. They knew he was bringing his own wife with him to that meeting, and they obtained a department store mannequin, which they slipped into his bed. Only the mannequin's face, blond wig, and exposed bosom were visible above the sheets. The Lothario entered the room first, carrying their luggage, caught a panicky glimpse of what he supposed was a naked blonde awaiting him as per appointment, and turned tail to run before his wife could get into the room. He wasn't speedy enough. They said the man spent the remainder of the convention trying to explain the joke, and his obvious guilt, to his wife. They thought it hilarious.

Another in-group joke—which was repeated often, and chased away sleep—had to do with drinking. Drinking anything: ginger ale, orange juice, beer, or booze. Someone behind me initiated the joke or routine or whatever it was, someone seated beyond my sight at the rear of our non-smoking section. I would hazard the guess that he was an oldster, to judge by the sound of him; he didn't wheeze or crackle or anything like that, but he was older than those others in the crowd. It began when the steward-esses distributed the first glass of orange juice, a practice they continued without stopping during the entire twenty-hour flight. The elderly voice behind me shouted: "Smoooth!" And in the next moment sixty hands shot into the air, sixty mouths gulped their juice, and sixty voices shouted out the reply: "Smoooth!" *That* continued all the way to Sydney.

Who could sleep?

But I used the long interval to get acquainted with Joe Karns and he with me. I learned that he was a Stateside newspaper reporter now serving as a travel writer, and at the same time attending the convention. He didn't seem too happy in the double duty, but I didn't ask the cause of his unhappiness. When he mentioned the Sydney hotel in which he and the group would be staying for a few days before going on to Melbourne, I managed to light a spark of interest in him when I told him that the hotel was a new and modern establishment, almost a copy of the plush American hotels, but that it was situated in the very center of Sydney's red light district. I said that if a visitor wished to visit the city's famed El Alamein Memorial Fountain down Darling-hurst Road, he—the visitor—was first obliged to run a gantlet of provocative ladies waiting on numerous hotel verandas along the way.

He turned to me and asked: "Why?"

Perhaps I misunderstood him, perhaps my reply was flippant. "The Australian free enterprise system, I guess."

I advised him to stock in a supply of groceries and liquids if he was staying there more than a day. Unlike American hostelries, the Sydney hotels had a refrigerator in every room while the restaurant prices tended to be on the high side because of the unfavorable rate of exchange. Taxi prices were quite low, compared to American cities, but other services were unusually high.

Eventually he got around to asking about me, about my presence on the aircraft. I was seated amid those sixty science fiction fans and I suppose I stood out like a bandaged thumb. Somewhat square. I told him about bamboo and bamboo mites. I am a botanist attached to one of the government agencies in the greenbelt near Washington, and this was my third trip down under.

Several years before, the government of the Northern Territory, Australia, decided to grow bamboo in that territory's near-tropical climate. I never understood why they made that decision, but at any rate they committed a large sum of money and launched an experimental program. It was a failure, a very costly failure. Like most bureaucracies they could not admit their mistake to the public without first spending additional millions in an attempt to learn the reasons for the failure, and in that search they contacted Washington. That brought me into the problem and I made my first flight to Australia. On this same airline, with gallons of orange juice.

I soon found the reason for the failure. No one in the government, including those on duty at the experimental station outside Darwin, realized the dual nature of bamboo.

Bamboo, like banana plants (not trees), are of the male and female genders. All attempts to grow bananas in California, Texas, and Florida were failures because the would-be growers had not taken gender into account. Both male and female banana shoots must be carefully cultivated and grown together in a common grove, awaiting that future year when nature—wind and insects—distribute the necessary fertilization from one plant to another. A given grove, a given area, can produce bananas and become self-perpetuating only after several years of careful husbandry.

The same basic rule applies to bamboo.

The government of the Northern Territory had selected only the sturdiest bamboo stock for transplanting, not realizing *that* bamboo was female. The weaker, male stock was left behind as unworthy. A costly failure was the result of that biological ignorance. I persuaded the experimenters to bring in and plant the weak male species alongside the sturdier female stock. Then, to hasten the growing process, to save several tedious years of waiting for Australian nature to produce healthy yields, I also persuaded them to import several thousand (of both sexes!) bamboo mites from Borneo. Bamboo mites, little known except in biological circles, provide the fastest and most reliable means of growing bamboo. The Borneo mite, in particular, is an excellent choice for cross-fertilization because of the mites' own agility and fecundity.

The experiment worked, as I learned when I made the second trip to the Northern Territory a few years later. The experimental station was then growing a healthy second-generation crop of bamboo, and I could agree with their estimate that in another two years the crop would be ready for harvesting on a commercial basis.

Now, today, I was making a third trip to Australia because a disaster had struck. Only a few weeks earlier a killer typhoon had struck across the coast of the Northern Territory, very nearly wiping out Darwin.

The storm also wiped out the experimental station, wreaking havoc on the struggling bamboo crop. The crop itself was flattened and broken off, but the greater problem was the total loss of the mites. Quite literally, the typhoon had blown them away, blown them out to sea, or crushed or drowned them, uncounted millions of them. And so, I was going in for the third time to help them regroup and replant. Washington had made its usual offer of assistance when the typhoon struck, and someone in Darwin had asked for me.

The schedule would be set back a year or two, but after replanting and after importing still more thousands of mites from Borneo, Australia would soon be growing its own native bamboo for market.

Joe Karns had been making notes while I talked. He told me again—apparently forgetful—that he was working as a travel writer on this trip, and asked my permission to visit the station, interview the experimenters, and perhaps photograph the mites, all in my name—that is, he wanted permission to use my name for reference. I gave it, of course, and he said *that* would make his editor happy. The Stateside news services had carried nothing of the bamboo and mite matter, although the tragedy of Darwin and its population was well covered. And finally—after an awkward hesitation—he admitted that he hadn't known anything of male and female bamboo. Or bananas.

I replied that it wasn't surprising. Many people in my own discipline, those not working in my particular field, knew nothing of the genders.

He put away his notebook and the conversation turned back to science fiction and the activities of the fan group on board. Once during that long night the ship's captain came back to learn the cause of the noise, and asked the group to settle down so that the other passengers could sleep. He only wasted his breath and his time. By now, a few bottles of Bourbon and scotch were making the rounds of the non-smoking section, and even those passengers who were not a part of the group were chanting the familiar battle cry after each swallow.

I asked Joe what science fiction writers could possibly write about, now that man had landed on the moon and had put down landers on Mars. He was vague, but said he thought there were more planets out there somewhere. And I admitted that, for my part, I had not read science fiction after sampling one—just one —book. The volume itself had been interesting in a curious way but it hadn't generated a desire to read more.

Of course he was polite enough to ask, and I told him that one book had been the collected works of Charles Fort.

He fell silent and was quiet for so long that I thought he'd dozed off.

Joe Karns, his fans, and I parted company in the customs shed at the Sydney airport some twenty hours later. Some Australian —another fan, I suppose—met them there and got them all through customs without a single suitcase or backpack being opened for inspection. The customs people simply opened a new exit and swept them through and out, while the rest of us waited in line while they pawed through our luggage. I'd like to know how the Australian greeter managed that.

I've often wondered how their convention went, and whether

Joe Karns visited the Darwin station, and if the group had an equally happy—and noisy—time on the trip back to the States. I didn't see any of them again after they left the customs shed. I only hope I didn't annoy Joe Karns with my questions, or the dull recital of my work, or that one query I had first put to him. To the best of my memory, Charles Fort never mentioned wombats.

—Wilson Tucker

Jacksonville, Illinois

August, 1976

Charles Fort
Never Mentioned
Wombats

I

"Charles Fort Never Mentioned Wombats"

The first hint that Australia was in my future came last spring, about ten o'clock on a Friday night, to be exact. The hint was a wombat, and it appeared on my desk at the *Clarion*.

Not a toy wombat or even a stuffed wombat, but a real, snuffling, butting, confused wombat. At least I think it "appeared." All I know for sure is, I heard this whooshing sound, and when I looked around from the typewriter on the rollaway cart next to my desk, I found myself nose to hairy nose with this thing that looked vaguely like a fifty-pound woodchuck. Whatever it was, its beady eyes looked a trifle glazed, but I can't say that I blame it. Mine were probably a little glassy, too. Weird things tend to happen around me, but they're usually not quite this weird or this close.

I said "Urk!" or something equally incisive as I spasmed to my feet, knocking my chair over in the process. After putting as much distance between myself and the beast as I could without climbing over a couple of desks, I more or less calmed down and realized that what I should do was get a picture, which goes to show how your mind works if you're always on the lookout for something—anything—to fill a couple of Sunday Supplement pages every week. A big, hairy creature appears out of thin air on your desk, and you don't scream or run, although it's touch and go for a second. Instead, you take its picture, in hopes you can run the photo with maybe a silly season article—"Wombat Appears Mysteriously in Newspaper Office"—or maybe a zoological feature—"Giant Marsupial Rodent Native to Australia."

Luckily, I was prepared. After years of never being able to

find a *Clarion* photographer when I needed one, I'd taken to carrying an Instamatic just about everywhere I went. I even had a couple of flash cubes in my desk. The only problem was to talk myself into getting close enough to reach the drawer, which took maybe a minute, or possibly five. While I eased myself forward and cautiously opened the drawer and groped for the flash cubes, I was running through the musty warehouse of my mental storage bins, trying to recall where I'd seen an animal like that, and wishing, for probably the millionth time in the last ten years, that my eidetic filing system included some sort of index. Not surprisingly, I found the flash cubes before I found the name.

The creature almost backed off the desk at the first flash, but then it settled down, more or less, which is more than can be said for the piles of accumulated debris on my desk. The animal snuffled around interestedly, knocking an empty Coke bottle and a stapler to the floor, and then it began experimentally munching on a paste pot. It didn't even flinch as I continued to flash at it, but it did abandon the paste pot shortly and started nosing about in a stack of papers, sending most of them after the bottle and stapler. A couple of pencils followed, along with some unseen items that I couldn't identify from the clunks they made as they hit the floor.

I was standing back a half dozen feet, out of flash cubes and wondering what to do next, when I heard something behind me. It sounded like someone stumbling as she came to a sudden stop, and then I remembered Nancy. We had been coming out of a movie a couple of blocks from the *Clarion* building when this absolutely brilliant idea for the closing paragraph of my hot air ballooning article came to me, so naturally I had to rush right up to the office to get it down on paper before it vanished. To my surprise, Nancy hadn't objected. It had been six months since she had quit the *Inside-Outside* staff to become an editor at a local publisher of children's books, so she was already getting nostalgic twinges about the place and welcomed the opportunity to wander around her old haunts for a few minutes, which is what she had been doing while I had been in the throes of terminal creativity.

I moved back a few more feet, to the aisle where she was standing and staring, wide-eyed and silent.

"I give up," she said, her voice slightly shaky, "what is it?"

"A wombat," I told her, my mental dust bin having just that moment spit out a filler item photo the *Clarion* had run several months before.

"A what bat?"

"Wombat," I repeated, and took a couple of seconds to scan the mental image of the half dozen lines of type below the blurry picture. "An Australian marsupial that likes to burrow," I quoted. "Reputed to be harmless unless you stick your finger in its mouth."

Nancy shuddered, presumably at the thought of sticking a finger or anything else anywhere near the animal, let alone into it. Still, she moved a little closer, easing her way down the aisle between the desks.

"If it's Australian," she said after a moment, "shouldn't it be on the travel editor's desk?"

I think she was joking, but I couldn't be sure. Six months working with nothing but children's books can give your mind a strangely literal bias.

"I don't suppose *you* happened to see where it came from?" I asked as we watched from a relatively safe distance while more papers and books slid and thudded to the floor.

She glanced toward me, a definitely suspicious look on her not-quite-cherubic face. "It's your desk and your wombat," she said flatly.

"Can I take that to mean 'no'?" She *was* suspicious, I realized, and I can't say that I blamed her. The *Inside-Outside* staff had never been known for excessive solemnity, and their practical jokes did often tend toward the elaborate and slapstick.

She shook her head, her straight, blond hair brushing at her shoulders. "The first time I saw the thing, you were foofing it in the face with your camera. Are you trying to tell me that *you* don't know how it got there?"

I shrugged, knowing that I probably looked guilty, whether I was guilty of anything or not. My face, they tell me, is expressive, but it rarely expresses what I want it to. And to tell the truth, I couldn't be completely sure that I wasn't just the teensiest bit responsible. Odd things have been happening around me most of my life, and I've never been sure why, although every so often I start wondering if I don't have an "aura" of some sort hovering around me, sort of like the little unpronounceable guy's black cloud in *Li'l Abner*. Somebody even suggested once, with a more or less straight face, that my "luck" was some form of ESP, that I somehow "homed in" on weird happenings, the way some guy named Frank Tower apparently homed in on disasters. (He survived three shipwrecks, including the *Titanic* and the *Lusitania*, and who knows how many more he might've gotten involved in if he hadn't been blackballed as a "Jonah.") That same person suggested my homing instinct might have something to do with my equally odd memory, which is a sort of fading photographic. But whatever it is, if it exists at all, it isn't something I have any control over. If I had anything to say about it, I would certainly conjure up something better than a late-night wombat.

"I just looked around," I told Nancy, "and there it was."

She looked even more skeptical. "Just materialized out of thin air, did it?"

"Apparently."

She shook her head again. "Charles Fort never mentioned wombats," she said finally, "but why not? Fish from the sky would be a little old hat these days anyway."

I didn't laugh, which I think disappointed her, but somehow I didn't feel like it. The last time I'd had anything to do with this thin air stuff, it had been people who were appearing and disappearing in front of other people's eyes, including my own, and it had ended up in a couple of murders. This was a wombat instead of a man, but it still wasn't the sort of thing that made for inner serenity and peace of mind.

In the meantime, the wombat had adapted rather well to its new home. It had cleared the area of everything but the typewriter, a few stray sheets of paper, and a large eraser I'd been hunting since Monday. It probably wouldn't be of any use to me now, though, since Wombie had already bitten it in two and was contentedly munching on one of the pieces.

"Whether you believe it or not," I said finally, "I didn't have anything to do with this. The question is, what do we do with it?"

"Call the Humane Society?"

"Are they open at this time of night?"

"They have an emergency number you can call twenty-four hours a day. Or wouldn't you consider this an emergency?"

"It'll do till a real one comes along," I admitted. "But what do we tell them? They'll never come if we tell them there's a wombat on the fourth floor of the *Clarion*."

"You said it's harmless, didn't you? Maybe we can take it to them?"

"Since when did you ever take my word for anything? Besides, maybe it's a rogue wombat."

"Karns, do you have *any* idea what you're talking about? A *rogue* wombat?"

"Why not? What would *you* call a wombat that goes to newsrooms on its vacation?"

Nancy was looking at me more suspiciously than ever now. "You're sure you didn't—"

She stopped abruptly, her eyes widening and her mouth freezing in a half-open position. I was more than a little afraid to look around to see what had brought on this sudden stasis, but after a second or two, I managed.

The air around the wombat was beginning to shimmer, like heat waves over a distant summer highway. Gradually, the shimmering became more distinct, as though the air itself was somehow thickening. Then, from a spot near the end of the desk, just above the level of the wombat, a pair of hands appeared. Large, hairy hands with several inches of large, hairy arms attached. The hands grasped the wombat around its portly middle and lifted. The wombat started squealing and wriggling, and a second later, everything vanished—hands, arms, wombat, and shimmering air.

Surprisingly, neither Nancy nor I screamed, perhaps because we were too numb to make any sort of sound. We stared, and I could feel her hands on my arm. I was sure there would be several finger-shaped bruises showing by morning.

Then she gave a sort of nervous giggle. "Esther told me," she said unsteadily, "that dates with you were apt to be unusual."

"Are they gone?"

"I think so. Whew! That was close. Now come on, let's get out of here!"

"You're sure you don't—"

"No, I don't want to try it again! I never should've let you talk me into this idiocy in the first place. Now come on, before someone else wanders by."

"No one else will come by. Don't worry."

"I don't care! We could get in real trouble if anyone catches us, especially now! Haven't you seen the memos yet?"

"I've seen them. But what are they going to do? Send us home? Now quit being such a worrywart."

"That's easy for you to say. You've got all kinds of seniority. But me—I could end up anywhere!"

"All right, all right; if all you're going to do is fret, all right. But wasn't it worth it? Just to see the expressions on their faces?"

"What expressions? You know I can't tell one expression from another on these people. I can't even tell one face from another! Now are we getting out of here or not?"

"If you'll just hold on a second. This thing can't be turned off and left, just like that. There are procedures. You should know that. If I missed one of the steps, and something blew—well, then we'd really have reason to worry. Now just settle down and we'll be out of here, safe and sound, in a couple of minutes."

II

"We Don't Have *Everything* Figured Out Yet!"

The next hint about Australia was more direct. It was a couple of months later, in early June, and I'd had plenty of time to recover from the wombat. Mike looked up from his desk as I wandered past on my way back from lunch one afternoon.

"Karns," he said, "you're going to Australia."

Inertia kept me going another yard or two to my own desk, catty-cornered across the aisle from Mike's, and I sat down heavily.

"Why?" Which seemed a reasonable question, considering I'd never been sent beyond the state line before.

"Because Werner just exercised his option for early retirement."

Werner Hubbard was—or had been, according to what Mike had just said—the *Clarion* travel editor. His main problem was that he hated to travel, at least under the conditions imposed by the *Clarion*. He had been threatening to quit as long as I could remember, particularly when, every few months, they hustled him off on a whirlwind tour of some remote section of the globe and told him to come back with enough stories to spread out over the next five or six months.

My own reaction was mixed. I didn't object to a little expense-account travel, particularly now. I had just called Nancy again, and she had just hung up on me again. She'd been doing that regularly lately, ever since the Night of the Wombat, and she must have been talking to Esther and a few others, too, because my social life, never the greatest, was in a real slump. Still, expenses or not, Australia would not have been my first choice. And cranking out three or four dozen humorless articles describing tourist traps and native aboriginal festivals did not particularly grab me, either. At least they spoke English there, after a fashion, and my trick memory would eliminate the chore of taking notes. A key word or phrase jotted down to trigger the playback circuit was all it would take. And with my penchant for stumbling into things—like the wombat—I might even end up with something more interesting than the standard, stereotyped travel articles, which are usually read only by people who have already been there and who want to compare notes and feel good about all the things they saw that the writer missed entirely. Which maybe was another reason Werner was perpetually grumpy. After each article appeared, he'd get a half dozen calls, some from friends, some from total strangers, all wondering why, as long as he had taken the trouble to go to this or that place, he hadn't taken the time to go to this or that restaurant or look at this or that fabulous sight. If a caller was particularly obnoxious —from Werner's viewpoint—Werner would suggest the caller write an article himself and submit it to the *Clarion*. And if anyone was naïve enough to take him up on it, Werner would write a critique, explaining in loving and poisonous detail why such an article could never be published, even in a grade school newspaper. I could always tell when he was writing a letter like that. It was the only time I ever saw him smile.

"You leave in August," Mike said, apparently taking my thoughtful silence as enthusiastic acceptance. Which, in a way, it was. As far as Mike was concerned, anything short of threatening to quit was considered enthusiastic acceptance, and even a threat was considered acceptance as long as it wasn't actually carried out. "You'd better get moving if you're going to have your passport and everything in order by then. If you need any help," he went on, eying me in a way that made it very clear that the "if" was strictly an empty courtesy, "call on Werner. I'm sure he'll be glad to help you in any way he can before he leaves."

As it turned out, I needed all the help I could get. Australia is not the easiest place in the world to get into. Officials have been known (according to Werner, who may have just been trying to scare me) to refuse a visa to someone whose second cousin was a schizophrenic, which led me to wonder about someone with a first cousin whose wife was a Rosicrucian. But they either didn't find out about Cousin Sue, or they didn't classify Rosicrucianism in the same box with schizophrenia, because I eventually got my visa. I had to make a special trip to the Australian embassy in Chicago, but I finally got the go-ahead, and it took only eight weeks instead of the standard six months. Needless to say, I didn't tell them about the disappearing wombat or anything else like that. I hadn't, in fact, mentioned the wombat to anyone. My pictures had come out with all the clarity of a typical flying saucer photo, and I knew what happened to people who showed *those* around, even the ones that showed a lot of detail and looked reasonably authentic. My pictures showed only that there had been an unphotogenic something on my desk, but for all the detail you could make out, it might have been nothing more than a weird-looking Teddy bear, and I wasn't about to open myself up to the sort of comments *that* would have inspired. And then there was the fact that, from what little I'd been able to pry out of Esther and the others, Nancy was firmly convinced that I had done the whole thing with mirrors and/or a couple of accomplices.

In any event, I had kept my mouth shut and, surprisingly, nothing particularly startling had happened during the post-wombat months. In fact, by the time departure day rolled around, I was beginning to wonder if the whole thing hadn't been a hairy-nosed delusion. I was even beginning to entertain hopes that I had outgrown my alleged attraction for strange happenings. Still, I couldn't completely suppress the other, more unsettling feeling that the last few months had merely been the lull before the storm, that all the things that hadn't happened were sitting around somewhere just waiting for me to stumble into their midst.

Then, during the layover at the Los Angeles airport, as I wandered into one of the waiting rooms, I spotted something that changed the feeling to a near certainty.

The something was Kay Clarke.

She was black—well, dark brown, anyway—and about six feet tall if you didn't count the three-inch Afro she still sported. As usual, she was wearing a casual sweater and slacks and carrying a guitar case large enough to smuggle a non-magnetic midget onto the plane.

I should have been glad to see her. After all, she was not only good looking but bright (brighter than me, I often thought, but then consoled myself that maybe it was just a different kind of intelligence) and had enough enthusiasm for any ten normal humans. On the other hand, there was the reason that my vague "feeling" had suddenly switched to near certainty at the very sight of her. The last time we had met, people started getting killed all around us, not to mention vanishing into thin air, and we almost got ourselves zapped before we parted company. As I've said before, odd events seem to cluster around me, clamoring for attention, but when Kay is around, both the frequency and intensity of the events shoot right off the scale. Still, she was the only woman I'd ever met who was intrigued rather than put off by such things. In fact, she was the one who had come up with the "extrasensory homing instinct" suggestion last year, which had a certain insane logic that I hadn't been able to shake no matter how hard I tried.

I was faltering to a halt, debating whether I should greet her with open arms or duck behind the nearest pillar until she left, when the debate became academic. She spotted me.

"Joe! Joe Karns!" Her contralto voice, particularly when she was using her hailing volume, was somehow both raucous and seductive, if you can imagine a combination like that. Sort of like a sexy carnival barker, maybe. "What are *you* doing here?"

I veered in her direction, and when I got within speaking rather than shouting range, I told her I was going to Australia.

Her face lighted up even more. "Lovely! You must be taking the same flight we are."

"We?" I glanced around suspiciously, and a moment later my suspicions were confirmed. Clustered around a rack of paperbacks a dozen yards away was a gaggle of disconcertingly familiar—well, faces might be overstating the case, but just say beards and mounds of hair, although there were a few conventional-looking ones mixed in.

"Yes, a bunch of us are flying out to the Worldcon," Kay explained. "It's in Australia this year."

I'd suspected as much. I'd inadvertently attended the World

Science Fiction Convention the year before, and that's where I'd stumbled into all those disasters and near disasters. And as far as I was concerned, that group was pretty close to being a disaster all by itself.

I managed a weak smile. "Oh. Where? In Sydney?" Which was supposed to be my first stop, so logically that would be where they were holding the convention.

"No, Melbourne," she said, and I breathed a sigh of relief. I wasn't due in Melbourne for three or four days, and by then it might be over.

"Too bad," I said. "I've got to go to Sydney first, so I guess we won't be on the same flight after all."

She laughed, and it would have been a lovely sound under other circumstances. "So are we," she said. "We'll be in Sydney a couple of days, then take a train to Melbourne."

Of course. The feeling, which was already near certainty, was bucking for inevitability.

"I'm surprised you didn't know," Kay went on. "Didn't Don tell you?"

"Don?"

"Don Thompson. Remember? He works for the *Clarion*, too." There was a touch of good-natured (I think) sarcasm in the tone.

"Oh, him. Sure, I remember, and no, he didn't tell me. But, then, I haven't seen that much of him since last year."

She sighed. "That's the trouble with the world these days. Filled with huge, impersonal corporations. Nobody talks to anybody, and they wonder why things get screwed up. Just think of all the money they could've saved if they'd only—"

"No, they couldn't have!"

I looked up just in time to see Don ambling over, having apparently detached himself from the cluster around the paperback rack. Don Thompson is a police reporter for the *Clarion*, and he spends most of his time hanging around police stations, logically enough, which explains why he isn't at the office very often, even less than I am. He looked like he'd lost a couple of pounds since the last time I'd seen him, and he was beginning to look square instead of chunky. Or maybe it was just that he was not wearing his usual plaid sport jacket, just a plaid sport shirt. He also appeared to have lost a couple of hairs, which he could ill afford, but he seemed to be trying to make up for the loss by letting what was left curl around his ears. I probably shouldn't say anything, though, since my own anachronistic crew cut was getting a little shaggy around the edges.

He came to a halt next to Kay, the top of his head almost reaching the level of her ear lobe. He was grinning evilly at me.

"They couldn't have what?" I asked.

"Don't try to sound so innocent, Karns," he said. "I knew all about Werner, and I knew what would happen if anyone knew I was going to Australia on my vacation."

"But they'd pay your expenses if—"

"Sure they would! If they knew I was going anyway, the best they'd do is pay half, and probably not that much, especially if they found out we were getting a group discount for everything. And they'd have me spending all my time talking to kangaroos or something equally fascinating. No, thanks. No way."

I suppressed an impulse to make a disparaging comparison of kangaroos and science fiction fans, but I knew pretty much what he meant. Tom Stratton had let it slip one year that he had finally saved up enough to go to Europe, and Werner had conned him into doing it "for him and for the *Clarion*." Tom did get about half his expenses paid (but none of his wife's), but he only got to see about a quarter of what he had planned to see. And he had had to report in to Werner's boss every other day, just to reassure him that he hadn't gotten lost and that he was, indeed, taking enough notes for the requisite number of articles. That sort of thing tended to take the fun and spontaneity out of a vacation.

"Besides," Don was continuing, sounding pleased with himself, which was not unusual, "I can afford it this year. Bob and I picked up a little extra money for those stories in the *Midnight Inquirer*. I don't suppose you saw any of them?"

"Bob?"

"Bob Adams, remember? The guy who kept disappearing last year?"

That Bob. Of course, who else? "I remember, but I didn't think *you* believed in him."

"Who has to believe in anything? Besides, the disappearing act isn't what we wrote about. You sure you didn't see the stories? A three-part series. 'My Brother Tried to Frame My Corpse for a Triple Murder!' "

I blinked. Now that I'd been reminded, I did remember the series, or the headlines for one installment, at least. I'd seen it as I'd been going through a supermarket checkout lane a few months before. "That was you?" I asked.

He shrugged modestly. "Bob's story, of course. I just helped him write it. And fill in a few extra details."

Kay was shaking her head in mock sadness. "Don, you never told me about that side of your sordid career."

He chuckled, a sound that went right along with his recurrently evil smile. "I'd thought about doing one on your empathy with audiences, your alleged 'emotion reflecting.' Maybe I'll try it when we get back. 'The Woman Who Turns On Hundreds of Men a Night!' Might be good publicity for you, Kay . . ."

"Sure it would! Next thing, you'll want me to do a centerfold for *Sing Out*." Abruptly, she glanced at her watch. "Come on," she said. "I don't want to miss the plane."

I started to say we had plenty of time, but before I could get the words out, I was being swept along in her wake, along with the rest of the more or less motley group that had been slowly drifting over from the paperback racks. Kay was like that. She generated a whale of a wake.

The plane wasn't ready, of course, but when we sat down to wait, Kay got into a discussion with a character sporting a square-cut, reddish-gray beard and a big mustache. Mostly they talked about the social significance of some book called *Evil Is Veil Spelled Sideways,* which I gathered was anticlerical one way or another—if it existed at all. I don't think they were serious, but it's sort of hard to tell when you haven't the faintest idea what they're talking about and you're trying your best to look as though you weren't associated with the group at all.

Eventually we were allowed to board, and when the elderly redbeard paired off with a suspiciously conventional-looking, similarly aged character who kept making bad jokes about being either a virgin flyer or a flying virgin, I managed to grab a seat next to Kay. A pleasant but harassed-looking woman with prematurely white hair seemed to be more or less—mostly less—

in charge, and it didn't take long watching that group milling around to see what had caused the white hair. The bespectacled character who claimed never to have been on a plane before kept intoning "Smo-o-o-o-th!" at irregular but frequent intervals. It appeared to be some sort of ritual, but I was afraid to ask Kay what it meant. I was also afraid that other people might join the refrain, and I was right. Pretty soon there was a deafening chorus every time anyone took a drink from a series of bottles that were being passed around continuously or whenever the plane banked or hit a downdraft.

Eventually, though, everyone got settled to a degree. Don was right across the aisle from Kay and me, and Bob Adams, Milquetoasty as ever, was next to him.

"Incidentally," Kay said not long after takeoff, "I think I've figured out how he does it."

"How who does what?" I asked. A reasonable question, considering she had been talking about an ill-fated novelization of *King Kong* about five seconds before.

"How Bob disappears, what else?"

What else, indeed. "You mean he's got it under control now?" I asked.

She shook her head. "Hardly. What I mean is, I figured out what must happen when he disappears. He doesn't *really* disappear at all."

"I told you that all along," Don commented smugly.

"That's not what I mean," Kay retorted. "He disappears but he doesn't—*disappear*. I mean, that would be impossible. If he just became transparent, his clothes would still be visible, for one thing. For another, even if he could make his clothes transparent, too, it wouldn't make any difference. The big problem is, if he actually became transparent, his eyes would be transparent, too, and he'd be blind."

Don shrugged, as if he knew what she was talking about and as if it only re-enforced his own case of terminal skepticism. As for me, it took a couple of seconds, but I eventually caught on. You see things because light hits all those rods and cones and things on your retina, thereby forming an image. If you, including your retinas, were transparent, light would go right through, presumably with no effect at all.

I was beginning to agree with Don. It had all been my imagination. "So how does he do it, then?" I asked.

"It's some kind of telepathy," Kay said. "He makes you *think* he isn't there. Instant hypnosis of a sort. You know how hypnotized people see what the hypnotist tells them to see rather than what's actually there."

"In other words," Don said, "he clouds men's minds. Does he also look for evil lurking in the hearts of men? And go sniffing around for bitter fruit?"

"I suppose you've got a better explanation?" Kay challenged.

"Aren't group-rate delusions good enough? And what about his late brother? He probably just made you *think* he vanished and reappeared a mile away, right?" Don's tone was still sarcastic.

"Well, we don't have *everything* figured out yet," Kay admitted. "But there's an explanation, don't worry."

"I don't, believe me. I haven't lost the least bit of sleep over your wild fantasies." He shook his head sadly. "Boy, it's you gullible types that give the rest of us a bad name. Just because you read science fiction doesn't mean you have to believe every crackpot story you come across."

"Believing your own eyes isn't being gullible," Kay said. "You probably agree with that hairy magician who was picking on Bob." Kay was starting to sound genuinely irritated; there was apparently still something about the mousy Bob Adams that brought out her maternal, protective instincts. "What was that little faker's name? The Amazing Horny or something like that?"

"And why shouldn't I agree with him?" Don asked condescendingly. "He duplicated the trick, after all, and—"

"But with Bob it isn't a trick!"

"So you say. Well, whatever it is, a couple of magicians did the same thing Bob allegedly did, and they did it under controlled conditions. Bob wasn't even able to flicker."

"Of course not! He has to be frightened for it to work! You know that! Those magicians may be dumb, but they're not frightening!"

"Yes, it *was* rather difficult," Bob Adams said apologetically into the momentary silence. "I kept telling them it only worked when I was scared, and all they did was try to calm me down."

He wagged his balding head back and forth slowly. "I don't think they really understood."

"Yes, the paranormal can be a very difficult field to study," came a cultured voice from across the aisle and just behind us.

I looked around to see a nominally black but actually light tan man, several shades lighter than Kay, middle-aged, tall, balding, with a hairline mustache, dressed in a conservative gray suit. He was eying us solemnly, somehow giving the impression of looking through an invisible monocle.

"When I was working with Dr. Rhine," he went on once he had our attention, "we achieved some rather startling results, though. Many of the most unusual were not reported, I'm afraid, because the subjects were unable to repeat their feats on command." A look of sadness darted across his face but was gone in an instant. "Also, Dr. Rhine was regrettably lax about his statistics. I'm sure that Lobachevsky would not have approved. In fact, Nick once told me— But I digress. I was saying that paranormal abilities, while difficult to prove under controlled conditions, remain a realm of fascinating possibilities."

Kay looked interested, although somewhat skeptical. "You actually worked with Dr. Rhine? What's he like?"

That was enough to set our new friend off on an hour of sparkling reminiscences. He'd obviously missed his calling. He claimed only moderate success at a dozen different, unrelated occupations, but his proper field was obviously a radio or TV talk show guest.

Even with such a stream of anecdotes, though, an occasional break was required, if only to ward off paralysis due to cramped seats. It was during one of my periodic perambulations up and down the aisle that I found myself in a minuscule "lounge" at the front of the plane. I'd been attracted by the familiar sound of a typewriter, and I'd halfway hoped to find an island of businesslike sanity in the cubbyhole, but I realized I was wrong the moment I stuck my head inside. There was a typewriter all right, but it was surrounded by a half dozen of Kay's group, seemingly all talking and laughing at once and occasionally fighting over whose turn it was at the keys.

Don, who had abandoned Rhine's assistant after only a few minutes, was also observing whatever was going on. Against my better judgment, I asked him what they were doing.

"Putting out a one-shot, of course. What does it look like?"

I didn't tell him what I thought it looked and sounded like, just asked what a one-shot was.

"A fanzine with only one issue," he explained, none too patiently. At least I remembered from last year that a fanzine was an amateur magazine of sorts, so I didn't have to ask for a translation of that. "They're just typing the stencils now," he said. "They'll run copies when they get to Sydney."

"What's it for?" I couldn't help asking, even though I realized I was beginning to sound like the straight man in a badly scripted training film.

"For the fun of it, of course," Don explained.

I had to admit, they did seem to be having fun. Then, as I was about to slip away, totally unnoticed, I realized, to my surprise, that they were talking about something I actually recognized. I couldn't imagine why or how it had gotten started, but they seemed to be staging a Tom Swifties revival. I hadn't heard one of those since I'd gotten out of high school, and the only ones I could remember were simple things like, "Let me out of this refrigerator," said Tom, coldly. Everyone in this bunch, though, was trying to outdo everyone else in making up obscure and/or complicated ones. They had even divided the things into different "levels" of complexity, although I never was able to figure out just what the criteria for the different levels were.

"Third level," someone shouted, and then went on: "'You're much too small to play a regular position on our hockey team, but there *is something* we could use you for,' said Tom, puckishly."

This was greeted by an equal mixture of groans and laughter and a sudden clatter of the typewriter.

"Second level," someone else yelled. "'I lost my watch in that tomb back there,' said Tom, cryptically."

More groans and typing, and an answering shout: "Watches don't 'tic' without a 'k.'"

"Don't be picky," someone else said. "But how about this? 'That tomb scared me so badly, I think I've developed a twitch.' Or do you spell that kind of tic with a 'k,' too?"

A deceptively innocent-looking blond girl laughed evilly. "Second level," she announced. "'Think nothing of it; I *like* to unclog drains this way,' said Tom . . . ?" She looked around expectantly. There was some general muttering, but no real answers. "Give up? 'Succinctly,' of course."

Even I groaned at that one, and decided to leave before my mind was entirely rotted away. Back at the seat, the raconteur was finally getting around to introducing himself as Denver Cross. He wasn't, he said, a fan, but a representative of a pocket calculator firm that was considering entering the Australian market.

"Although I do read science fiction now and again. I never did try to write it, unfortunately. Horace asked me to submit a piece when he started *Galaxy*, but I was really too busy at the time. There was this dealer in Mexican jade who . . ."

It looked like a long trip, no matter which end of the plane I was in.

"Are you sure you know what you're doing, Artil?"

"Of course! I've been researching these humans, in depth, and I know how they think."

"For half a period! That's hardly long enough to become an expert."

"Don't worry. Just look at this stuff. Space travel, alien invasions, time travel, psi powers, everything! And you should see their visual entertainments! They're accustomed to it, believe me. They've been conditioned to it most of their lives."

"Just remember, you're the one who's up Excrement River if it doesn't work."

"Up what, sir?"

"You can ask that? And still claim to know these people? Haven't you even studied the language update tapes?"

"Yes, sir, of course, but—"

"Never mind! Just get back out there, Artil, and make very, very sure that nothing does go wrong! Remember, you're the one—"

"I know, sir. Excrement River. Yes, sir."

III

"What Did He Do, Unravel a Brillo Pad?"

As I had suspected, it was indeed a long trip. Even on the rare occasions when I managed to get out of earshot of both the one-shot producers and the multi-talented computer salesman, I kept getting cornered by a gabby botanist who insisted on explaining the sex life of bamboo to anyone who'd listen without making openly derisive sounds, which pretty well limited his audience to me. And to make matters worse, he somehow got the idea that I was connected with Kay's group, so that when he wasn't lecturing about bamboo, he was babbling on about what a "fascinating subculture" I belonged to.

As I said, a long trip, not to mention a strange one, but despite occasional doubts, we did eventually reach Sydney. Or so the pilot told us over the PA system, and since there was enough daylight left for us to recognize its two main travel brochure landmarks, I was willing to take his word for it. From that height, however, the Sydney Harbour Bridge looked much like any other long bridge, and the impossibly expensive and acousti-cally disastrous (according to some obscure article) Sydney Opera House looked like a couple of toy paper sailboats that had run aground. I tried to imagine what the opera house interior looked like, but had no luck whatsoever. Probably a lot of waste space, like a '59 Chevy's tail fins, which a couple of the sections resembled if you looked at them from the right angle.

On the ground, I was expecting a long, tedious wait to get through customs, but a large Australian with an even larger beard and a ghastly fluorescent sweater labeled "Aussiecon" seemed to have greased the skids, and we were passed through with only a cursory check. Don and Kay obligingly escorted me through with them, explaining, in a well-mixed gesture of help-fulness and sadism, that I was the group's mascot. Then we were through and ready to move on to where buses were waiting to take us to our hotels. As I might have expected, in spite of the fact that there were dozens of hotels in Sydney, I was booked into the same one Kay's group was in. From Don's inscrutably amused look when this was discovered, I wasn't sure if it was my serendipity operating again or his undercover machinations back at the *Clarion.*

We were clustered around the buses when a tall, gangling young man with some kind of broad and curly brimmed army hat, an astoundingly full beard, and an incomprehensible dialect appeared next to Kay and started talking to her. I caught about every third word, but I eventually figured out that he was telling us there were more fans than seats in the buses, but that he would be ecstatic if he were allowed to chauffeur a few of us himself. Kay, who seemed to have an ear for dialects, translated for the rest of us and introduced him as an Australian fan named Irv Radsack and asked if I wanted to pile in with them. To tell the truth, I'd been thinking about a taxi, but then I thought about justifying the fare on my expense account and de-cided to go along with them. The only one who objected strenuously to the free ride was Don, but when it became clear that it was either Radsack's Holden or a taxi, he gave in, albeit with poor grace and great reluctance.

As the four of us, Kay, Don, Adams, and myself, trailed after Radsack, Kay explained that he was a neofan, which I gather meant that he had just discovered fandom recently. She didn't say what else he was, but I was getting used to that. As I had found out at the Worldcon I'd stumbled into last year, fans were rarely identified by the work they did or the profession they belonged to—unless, of course, that profession happened to be writing in one form or another. Instead, they're tagged as being from a particular city, having published a particular fanzine, being associated with this or that sf convention, or being en-gaged in a bitter feud with this or that person or group—or sometimes with 99 per cent of the rest of fandom. But never as a salesman, an engineer, an executive, a carpenter—nothing like that. For instance, I remember Don explaining to someone on the plane: "Oh, him. You know. He and What's-His-Name put on the Rubi-Con a couple of years ago. He's been fighting with Larry ever since. Didn't you see his letter in *Yandro* last year?" (*Yandro*, according to Don, was a sort of Galápagos tortoise among fanzines, having plodded along the beaches of fandom under its hard-shelled editor since practically the dawn of civilization.)

In any event, Radsack was new to the sf scene, hadn't had anything to do with conventions, and wasn't fighting with anyone yet. I had no idea what he did in the outside world, but my guess was that he at least *wanted* to be a Sydney tourist guide, probably for owls or bats. The sun was already touching the horizon by the time we had all been shoehorned into Radsack's elderly Australian-made Holden, but Radsack, as soon as he pulled out into traffic, peeled off in the opposite direction from the other carload of fans I thought we had been following.

"You'll want to see somewhat of Sydney," he explained when Kay and Don protested that it had been at least twenty-four hours since anyone had gotten more than a few brief naps on the plane. "Can't let Melbourne have all the glory. Good practice for the con, too," he added cheerfully as he headed west, directly away from where Kay's bilingual—English and Japanese—tourist map said the hotel was. "You certainly don't plan on much sleep there, eh?"

I almost protested that I wasn't even going to the convention, but I stopped before more than a word or two had emerged. I wasn't sure why I stopped. The only reason I'd "joined" the group was to get through customs. Now that I was through, there was no reason why I shouldn't ditch the whole lot of them. Except maybe for Kay. Still, I didn't say anything. A life of serendipity—i.e., sitting back and waiting for things to happen—is not good preparation for dealing with forceful personalities.

During the next hour, whenever we managed to force our eyes open, we were treated to shadowy forms that were, according to Radsack, such inspiring sights (if we could only see them in the daylight) as the town hall, a couple of cathedrals, and a cenotaph or two. It wasn't so much a Cook's Tour as it was a scullery maid's tour, and we all began to protest when Radsack approached the harbor bridge, which we were afraid meant that he might be done with Sydney proper and was about to start on the rest of Australia. Instead of crossing the bridge, though, he swerved into a series of waterfront streets that ran by and sometimes under the bridge, and finally started in the general direction of the hotel.

Don, meanwhile, had been getting more nervous and irritated by the minute, and I could see him working up to either leaping from the car or taking a poke at Radsack—probably at his belt buckle, since it was doubtful he could reach the Australian's chin and, even if he could, there was no guarantee he could find it amidst the beard. Kay, however, seemed to be getting into the spirit of things, drowning out Don's complaints and worries with a few unaccompanied but rousing verses of something called "The Road to Gundagai," or maybe "We Camped at Lazy Harry's," I was never sure which. I did, though, recognize the tune of "Take That Night Train to Memphis" despite the fact that the words had been warped into "Take That Night Tour of Sydney." Adams, of course, simply sat in the corner and watched and listened, as did I in the opposite corner. After all, the *Clarion* was paying me for travel articles, and I was certainly being exposed to sights, dimly lighted though they were, that your average tourist would never see. Probably he'd never want to see them, but that was another problem altogether.

But it was about then, as we were cruising along a deserted street in an industrial area, large warehouse-like buildings looming up on both sides in the misty rain that had begun to fall, that I suddenly realized that what I'd been suspecting for the last twenty-odd hours was indeed true: The things that hadn't been happening around me during the last few months had been lying in wait for me somewhere. And the somewhere was here.

A half block ahead of us, a door in one of the massive buildings flew open. Even in the car, I could hear the door as it slammed back against the wall. In the same instant, a man charged through the door, tilted so far forward that it was a wonder he didn't fall on his face as he ran. The light from the street lamps at the corners wasn't good and the windows were partly fogged over, but I could see that he was dressed in solid black. Even his hands were covered with dark gloves.

He reeled to a stop in the middle of the street, almost directly in front of us. He was huge, like a pro basketball center who could double as a wrestler. Not a real giant, maybe, but he could have played the Frankenstein Monster without platform shoes. He looked around, his head moving unevenly, like a poorly controlled puppet. His eyes swept past our car and looked back at the door through which he had just appeared. Then, in a double-take that was so perfect it seemed staged, the face turned back toward our approaching car.

Radsack had already hit the brakes and was swerving to the right, toward the far side of the street and away from the apparition on the center line. He was muttering something under his breath, the first time in the last hour that he hadn't been explaining loudly and enthusiastically what our beautiful surroundings would look like if only we could see them during the day.

Then there was a motion in the doorway. Nothing more came charging out, but inside, in the blackness, something moved. I couldn't tell what it was, and before I could get a better look, the car was swerving again and I was lurching against Don.

When my eyes refocused, I saw that the black-clad behemoth, being either very desperate or very trusting, had leaped directly in front of the car and was waving his hands wildly. Radsack, probably unsure as to whether the giant or the Holden would either one survive a collision, twisted the wheel back to the left, and a second later we thudded into the curb. Luckily, despite the misty film on the pavement, we had slowed enough by then so that all we got was a shaking up as the front wheels hit the curb, bounced backward, and stopped.

We were barely ten feet from the man, who looked even larger and more threatening at this distance, and less than fifty from the still-open door beyond him. I could see now that his features were craggy, but somehow the total face looked rounded, with full lips and eyes like Bela Lugosi's on a good night, sort of glittering. And his hair looked like a short Afro, very thick and kinky, except it was golden. Not blond, even in the dim light, but golden, as if it'd been sprayed with Day-Glo paint. His clothes were a little more normal—black slacks and a dark, heavy turtleneck sweater, and dark gloves.

Radsack seemed frozen now that the car had stopped. He was

gripping the wheel as if he were trying to crush it, not turn it, and he was making no motion toward the shift lever. Don, however, was another matter. The uneasiness and irritation that had been surfacing more and more frequently ever since we had arrived at the airport suddenly erupted in a rapid-fire tirade.

"Is this your idiot idea of a joke?" he demanded, his voice pitched a notch higher than normal. "Aussiefandom's way of welcoming innocent Yankees? If it is, I can tell you I don't think much of your script or that Harpo Marx wig your friend out there is wearing! What did he do, unravel a Brillo pad?"

Radsack only shook his head helplessly, and the man outside, suddenly exploding into motion, vaulted across the hood of the car and grabbed the driver's side door handle in his huge, gloved hand. I was on the same side, in the back, and I was beginning to feel a bit panicked, although there wasn't much of anything I could do about it except wish fervently and futilely that Radsack would come to life enough to get us moving again. And my upstairs observer, that useless little chunk of schizophrenic detachment that sits around in the back of my mind most of the time, was starting to look around interestedly. As usual, he/it offered no useful suggestions, just looked and made silent and pointless comments about the utter absurdity of what was going on. I keep telling myself that he's just an odd corner of my own mind, but there are times when I wonder, particularly when he steadfastly refuses either to go away or do something even remotely useful.

Then the door was wrenched open. From the grating sound it made, I figured it must have been locked, although I suppose it could have been badly rusted hinges. Then, as the giant released the door, a huge, black-gloved hand reached inside and grasped Radsack's arm. Radsack was tall, but he obviously lacked the bulk and power of the other. He hung onto the wheel until I was sure the steering column would have to bend, but then the hands let go with a snap and Radsack was hauled out of the car like a reluctant cork from a bottle. An instant later, the giant forced himself inside, wedging himself behind the wheel, his knees up and spraddled like a kid on a tricycle that's too small.

"Is that you, Gillespie?" Don was shouting. "You wearing elevator shoes, you cretin? You're not *that* big!"

The giant, sitting motionless as his eyes roamed rapidly over the dashboard, paid no attention. Kay, in the front seat, was finally scrambling for the door handle but not finding it. Don began pounding the giant on the back of the head with his fists, but the assault was ignored as the giant suddenly came to life and jammed the shift lever into "Drive" and floored the accelerator. The Holden lurched forward, barely missing Radsack, who was staggering to his feet in the street.

As the car shot past the darkened doorway, there was once again motion deep within it, a darker something within the darkness of the door itself.

The engine fell silent.

One instant we were accelerating down the street, the engine roaring, and the next there was only silence and coasting. The giant slammed on the brakes, throwing everyone forward, battered the door open, and managed to lunge sideways out of the car, still ignoring Don's yelling and pounding.

Whirling, the giant leaned down toward the car, jabbed his hand in through the open door, grabbed my wrist, and pulled. It was totally unexpected, especially since I was in the back seat, and the only thought I had was that he must've thought it was me who had been pounding at his head instead of Don. But all I had time for was the thought. There was no time to brace myself or anything else as I was yanked over the back of the front seat like a rag doll. Kay made a belated grab but managed to do nothing more helpful than rip a button off my back pocket, and my own momentary grip on the door frame resulted only in what felt like a couple of sprained fingers.

For a moment I was flying through the air, and then a huge arm came around to clamp me to the giant's side, and I was being carried, face down, tucked under one arm like a 160-pound football. I flailed around wildly, landing a couple of awkward blows to his stomach, but I quit when I realized it felt like I was hitting a huge lamppost.

Then, as suddenly as the car's engine had quit a few seconds before, the giant's engine quit. His left foot thudded to the pavement, but instead of straightening and driving the huge body forward again, it continued to bend, seemingly in slow motion. For once, my upstairs observer had a timely and practical suggestion: Cover your head, you idiot, before you get it splattered all over the concrete!

Luckily, the warning was superfluous. As my captor fell, he twisted sideways so that he came down on his side, with me on top of him, not on the bottom. An instant after he struck the ground, his grip loosened, and I frantically scrambled away, on all fours at first, then lurching to my feet when I was out of his reach.

Kay and Don had by then piled out of the Holden and were converging on me, along with Radsack. Kay got to me first and put a supporting arm around my shoulders, which was an excellent idea. My legs, I suddenly discovered, were a trifle rubbery.

"Are you all right?" she asked.

"More or less," I said, trying to take inventory. The fingers didn't quite feel sprained after all, but they didn't feel all that good, either. "But we'd better—"

"Here! Come here you must!"

The voice was little more than an urgent, hoarse whisper. The giant was struggling to raise himself on his elbow. His face, outlined harshly by the still-burning headlights a dozen yards away, was pale, almost chalky. The only life was in the eyes, which reflected the headlights like a cat's.

One hand was extended toward us, and I drew back involuntarily as something glinted in his palm. My first thought was of a weapon, but then, as the hand opened wider, I saw that it was only a disk, a pale gray, two-inch-wide disk, and I relaxed, relatively speaking.

But then I got a better look at his hand, now outstretched and flat. Judging by the sudden tightening of Kay's grip on my arm, she must have gotten an equally good look.

The hand—the black-gloved hand that reached out toward us urgently—had six fingers.

"Here!" the giant repeated, pushing the disk even further toward us. "Before too late it is!"

Don, who had halted several feet away, muttering loudly to himself, apparently also noticed the hand, and stopped in mid-mutter with his mouth open.

"What *are* you?" Kay whispered, obviously torn between a desire to run and a desire to get closer and ask endless questions.

Radsack came up then, still wobbling, and peered at the man's hand from a safe distance. "What's that he's got?" he asked.

"Take it you must!" The giant's voice was still only a hoarse whisper, but the sound cut like a knife, and his hand twitched as if he were about to fling the featureless disk toward us. "Failed have I, but—"

His eyes, still glistening in the glare from the headlights, darted toward the open doorway beyond the car, and his face seemed to grow even paler.

"Take it!" he repeated intensely. "Warn you it will when—" He seemed to struggle for a word, for a thought that wouldn't come.

Kay, with more nerve than I could muster at the moment, reached out and took the disk from the six-fingered hand. As she retreated with the disk clutched in her hand, the giant breathed a sigh of relief, then slumped to the pavement again, but his eyes remained fixed on her.

"Warn you it will when near they are!" he said, the whisper growing fainter. "A chance still there is, if you—"

Again his eyes shifted beyond us to the open door. "No time," he went on, still fading until we could barely make out the words. "Now go you must, quickly, before—"

Abruptly, even the whispering stopped, and the giant's arms moved weakly in the air, as if trying to ward off something that he knew could not be stopped.

The air around him wavered, shimmered.

Like the air around the wombat, I suddenly thought. All I needed now to make the insanity complete was a pair of gigantic hairy arms appearing out of nowhere.

But no arms materialized. Instead, the giant's body stiffened, and for a moment it seemed to rise from the pavement. It was only an inch or so, and it could have been the result of the muscles in his back tightening, arching his entire body, but the body appeared to remain straight.

Then he disappeared.

Literally, like the wombat, he disappeared, except without the hairy hands clutching him. I *think* his feet went first, but it was so fast I couldn't be sure. One second he was there, maybe five

feet away, stretched out on the wet pavement, the faint mist still
falling on him—on all of us—and the next second, he was gone.

For another second, the mirage-like shimmering remained in
the air where he had been, and then, with a faint whooshing
sound, it too was gone.

And from behind us, from somewhere near the door through
which the vanished giant had first appeared, there was a sound.
A humming, not quite like the sixty-cycle hum you can hear
close to a power line, but something like it, something that, word-
lessly and mindlessly, gave the impression of power—of power
about to be unleashed.

"Are you all right?"

*"Yes, I'm all right! Now is that it? Am I through with this
degrading nonsense?"*

*"Now, now, Verrmond, it couldn't have been all that bad. And
try to remember what is at stake."*

*"That's easy for you to say, just sitting back here safe and
sound, watching the rest of us out there making fools of ourselves. I'm telling you, Maurtiss—"*

*"I know, I know, and I have to admit, I don't like it all that
well myself. But we are committed to this plan of Artil's now, so
there's no point in bickering. After all, despite our differences,
this is a team effort—an exclusive team, I need not remind you,
but a team nonetheless."*

*"You needn't bring that up again! To tell the truth, I'm getting
a little fed up with all the secrecy around here, all the trickery. I
sometimes wonder—"*

*"Verrmond! Don't forget, you have as much to lose as the rest
of us!"*

*"I realize that, believe me. If I wasn't in so deep, do you think
I'd subject myself to this? This is not what I joined the Department for."*

*"We didn't force you into anything, certainly not into our own,
shall we say, inner circle. You were most eager, as I recall."*

*"I was younger then. I didn't—I certainly never thought it
would lead to anything like this!"*

"Now, now, we have to remain calm. Your part is finished, and

you did quite well. It will all be over in just a few days. Bondeach will be gone and we won't have anything to worry about."

"I hope you're right, Maurtiss, that's all I can say. I just hope you're right . . ."

IV

"That Clown Must've Taken Lessons in Hokey Dying"

Except for Don, who was shocked into mouth-gaping immobility, we ran, and Kay and I managed to drag Don with us, his feet barely touching the pavement. Radsack, too, recovered rapidly and was already in the Holden, grinding at the starter, when we arrived. Adams was still in the corner of the back seat, looking anxious and confused, and I was surprised that he hadn't vanished himself.

Then the engine caught, and we were all inside, Don only now beginning to mutter and resist. All the while, the humming was growing louder, seeming to come nearer. Involuntarily, our eyes went toward the darkened, empty doorway.

Only now it was neither completely darkened nor completely empty. There was something there, something that wouldn't come into focus, wouldn't stand still to be seen. It was all in shades of gray and black, but it reminded me of those formless, constantly shifting patterns that some movie theaters project on the screen during intermissions—except that here someone was also constantly fooling with the focus and never quite getting it right.

Our ears were beginning to hurt, and we could feel the vibrations in our bodies when Radsack finally got the car in gear and, after a momentary hesitation as the tires spun soundlessly on the wet pavement, tore away down the street.

We had tossed Don into the back seat next to Adams while Kay and I had jammed ourselves into the front, and now we twisted around to see through the back window. The door to the building, receding rapidly, was still shifting and pulsing like an out-of-focus thundercloud, but the humming had begun to fade as soon as the car had started to move.

It couldn't have been more than a few seconds before we reached the first intersecting street and Radsack cut across the street in a sliding right turn, but it seemed like forever. Then, an instant before our view of the door was cut off, it seemed that the movement within it stopped, and it became once more a simple, darkened opening in a huge, featureless building. At the same instant, the humming stopped, and, though it may have been my peripheral vision playing tricks, it seemed that the street lamp at the far end of the block momentarily dimmed.

As suddenly as it had started, it ended. As we moved out of sight of the door, it was as if we burst out of an invisible cocoon into open air. I felt weak as I twisted around in the seat again, becoming aware for the first time of the way Radsack and Kay and I were jammed together. It was surprising that Radsack had been able to move his long arms and legs enough to operate the car.

We slowed to a less frantic pace as Radsack let up on the accelerator. The world seemed to be slipping back into normal gear, but still we were all silent, as if we were afraid that a single word might plunge us all back into whatever it was we had finally emerged from. Another block went by, then two, and we were climbing a steep hill, then coming up on a broad, well-traveled, well-lighted street. The Holden rolled to a stop by the curb a dozen yards back from the busy cross street, and I could hear Radsack letting his breath out in a wheezing sigh.

"What happened?" It was Bob Adams, looking timidly and confusedly from one to the other of us.

Kay laughed suddenly, not quite explosively. "I wish I knew," she said quietly.

"Yeah!" Don was coming snappishly out of his trance at last. "How did you manage that, Radsack? It was a good show all right, but—"

"You think *I* arranged that?" Radsack twisted his head around toward Don, knocking his wide-brimmed hat—which somehow he still possessed—askew against the roof of the car as he turned. His tone and expression, what little could be seen peering through the beard, indicated an advanced case of incredulousness.

"You were doing the driving, Irv!" Don accused. "All that so-called sight-seeing must've just been a way to kill time until your friends got all the special effects prepared. 'Aliens are among us!' Really!"

"Come on, Don," Kay protested, "you saw that monster disappear right in front of your eyes."

"So? I've seen lots of people disappear right in front of my eyes. I wrote theater reviews one summer, and every other live show was a magician. I never spotted how they worked their tricks, but I knew it wasn't real. And I saw the Amazing What's-His-Name vanish last winter, remember? 'Duplicating' whatever it is you *say* Bob here does. No, that doesn't prove a—"

"In case you didn't notice, Don," I broke in, "the guy not only disappeared, he had six fingers."

Don stopped in midsentence, blinking, and I thought I saw a slight tremor sweep through him. His eyes twitched momentarily toward Radsack before settling back on me.

"Six . . . ?" Then, with an effort, he reverted to his normal self. "So what's new about that? There's a whole village in France like that." He looked thoughtful. "Of course," he continued, "if the extra pinkie or whatever stuck straight out and didn't do anything, it could mean he used to work for that idiot TV show about alien invaders. Remember all those zoom-in close-ups of stiff fingers, Kay?"

"How could I forget it? But this was *real!* And he—"

"That thing he gave you—do you still have it?" I asked.

She raised her hand, opening it slowly. She still had the disk. It was about two inches in diameter, maybe a quarter of an inch thick, and it was pale gray, like polished lead or maybe pewter. She turned it over; the two sides were identically featureless. Just a little round slab of metal.

"Quite a souvenir," Don scoffed. "I could work up something more alien-looking than that myself. Looks like a piece of scrap from a punch press. Add a couple of lights and you've got the same gadget they used on that other TV show—remember the one where the aliens ended up having a trampas walk down the street in some western ghost town?" He laughed sharply. "Whoever thought up this stuff sure didn't have much taste!"

During Don's tirade, I had taken the disk gingerly in my hand. It was perfectly smooth, almost slippery, with rounded edges; not something from a punch press, despite Don's opinion. It was also very light, so light it felt more like plastic than metal. I tried to play back what the giant had said at the last. "Take it you must. Failed have I, but—" Then another "Take it!" And finally, "Warn you it will when near they are. A chance still there is, if you— No time. Now go you must, quickly, before—"

I must have been muttering the words aloud as the playback went along, because when I looked up from the disk, everyone was staring at me.

Don snorted as I fell silent. "That clown must've taken lessons in hokey dying! And backward grammar. I haven't heard that many incompleted and incomprehensible sentences since my last Sherlock Holmes film festival! Really remarkable the way he managed to get cut off each time at just the right spot."

Radsack stared at him, shaking his head in disbelief, and Don pulled back momentarily. "My god, Thompson, you *really* think— I can't believe it, I just can't believe it!"

"Neither can I, Irv, neither can I." Don's words were nonchalant, even abrasive, but there was an undertone of nervousness that he couldn't completely conceal.

"But he was an alien," Radsack went on, "and he was apparently injured! Doesn't that mean anything to you? And he was trying to talk in a foreign language, on top of everything else. How coherent would *you* be under those circumstances?"

As Radsack spoke, I couldn't help but notice that *he* seemed noticeably more coherent than he had been when we had first run into him at the airport, although that may have just meant that my ears were getting to the point where they could filter out his accent. Maybe.

"Sure," Don was saying, "but he overdid it, and then some. What was it, three separate times he started something and stalled out in the middle? Come on, I've seen too many bad movies for me to miss something as obvious as that."

Radsack seemed totally flabbergasted by this last outburst and sat silently, shaking his head. Adams, raising a hand tentatively, like a shy kid in grade school wanting to leave the room, spoke into the silence in his usual, apologetic tone: "Shouldn't we really report this to the police?"

Don shot him a look that started out to be a withering putdown but quickly shifted to something else, like maybe understanding. I suspected that the *Midnight Inquirer* articles the two of them had collaborated on were not the last such things Don had in mind for Adams and himself. Or maybe the Milquetoasty Adams simply inspired tolerance and/or sympathy in people. Kay had certainly stuck up for him often and valiantly for no good reasons.

"The police? And tell them what?" Even with the visible effort, though, Don couldn't keep quite all the sarcasm out of his tone. "That we just saw a scene from a grade Z science fiction movie? What do we show them? The so-called 'victim' has vanished without leaving so much as a smudge on the street. All we've got is that two-headed—or no-headed—coin. And when the sergeant——or whatever they have over here—wants to know who we are, we tell him we're a bunch of science fiction fans from the States? No, thank you! Besides—"

He looked toward Radsack, who had turned to face him again and was leaning back in the crowded front seat, his hands pressing lightly against the wheel.

"Besides," Don went on, "as far as I'm concerned, this is just an elaborate 'welcome to Australia' show."

Again Radsack shook his head, the curl-brimmed hat brushing against the car roof. He didn't bother to look back. "I don't see how you can think— Look! Look at this door!"

Radsack worked the handle, and the door on the driver's side swung open with a grating noise and hung there, drooping slightly.

"This thing worked perfectly before that monster tore it out by its bloody roots! And for all your talk about magicians, you never saw anyone vanish in the middle of a city street!"

"So *you* think we should go to the police, too?" The sarcasm Don had partially suppressed in talking to Adams returned at full volume, but so did the undercurrent of nervousness. Whistling—or shouting—past the graveyard, I thought. Deep down, maybe Don was a believer, but he didn't really want to be, so he kept up this continual barrage . . .

"I didn't say that," Radsack said. "The authorities would simply think we were having them on."

"Then what? What do you, in your native wisdom, recommend?"

"I don't know. But the other fans, back at the hotel—"

"Oh, sure!" Don laughed sharply, nervously. "That would be just great! We go around telling everyone about it! That would *really* put the icing on the cake for you, wouldn't it? 'The Yanks really fell for it, Charlie. Just listen to them now.' Not on your life!"

Radsack stared at Don blankly, as if not sure what to make of the pugnaciously skeptical American, and to tell the truth, I wasn't all that sure what to make of him myself. I wasn't one of Don's closest friends by any means, but I thought I knew him at least a little. But his present display— I can't say it wasn't like him, because, in a way, it was. It was just that the degree and intensity had been stepped up. Don was normally skeptical and often enjoyed puncturing people's arguments and/or egos, but this seemed to go beyond anything like that, and I had the definite feeling that, whatever else was going on, Don wasn't enjoying himself.

"You *still* think that was staged?" Radsack's voice was a notch higher, and he glanced at the rest of us, as if seeking backing against the disbeliever.

"I believe it," Kay said, "but you do have to admit, it *was* pretty hokey."

When no one else spoke up, Radsack let his breath out in a whooshing sigh, turned to face forward in the seat again, and put the Holden in gear.

"All right," he said, as he pulled out onto the major street we had been facing for the last few minutes, "keep it to yourself or not. As for me, I am bloody well going to get to the bottom of this, one way or another."

At various times during the "discussion," I had thought of bringing up my vanishing wombat, but the thought had never gotten serious. My upstairs observer, who didn't really believe anything that had happened in the last half hour anyway, had wisely cautioned me against such foolishness, and for once I was in full agreement with him. Maybe later, when Superskeptic wasn't around, I might mention it, but not now.

Then I noticed that I still had the disk in my hand. I looked at it again but could still see nothing informative about it. As I handed it back to Kay, she shivered slightly but said nothing.

I settled back as best I could in the cramped confines of the Holden's front seat and tried to enjoy the sensation of being in such close quarters with Kay, but the effort was only marginally successful. Vanishing wombats and six-fingered giants kept wedging themselves between us.

"Well, Artil, what went wrong?"

"I don't know, sir. I just don't understand. Perhaps Verrmond—"

"Don't try to blame Verrmond! I watched his performance, and it was perfect! The entire display went off without a hitch. The only problem is those—those people you selected! What happened to that tremendous gullibility you were telling me about? It struck me as just the opposite, if you don't mind the observation."

"Actually, it was just the one, sir. The others weren't—"

"That one was enough! And the others didn't seem all that thoroughly convinced, either. From what you led me to believe, they should have been shouting it from the rooftops by now."

"They should have! I just don't understand it, sir. But next time—"

"Yes, Artil, next time! Just remember, those people are your responsibility! You selected them!"

"Yes, sir, but they seemed so—"

"I know how they 'seemed'! The problem is how they are! Now quit wasting valuable time calling in to make flimsy excuses! Understood, Artil?"

"Understood, sir . . ."

V

"An Abominable Pedestrian, Maybe?"

Somehow, we all got checked into the hotel, a twin-tower job right in the middle of the Sydney red light district, and I wondered once again if Don had had some undercover influence back at the *Clarion* in getting me reservations here. It might be more interesting than other hotels in Sydney, but I doubted that this was a good area for me to cover in any of the articles, no matter how interesting it turned out to be. The *Clarion* was, after all, a family newspaper, and a lot of the families were pretty stodgy, I gathered from the "Letters to the Editor" column. The *Clarion* didn't drop "Doonesbury" when they ran the gay sequence last year, but it was touch and go for a while. One more irate phone call probably would have tipped it.

As always, my upstairs observer spent a fair amount of time rationalizing away the evening's events while the rest of me checked in and made an attempt to get settled. One pleasant surprise, I discovered immediately, was that each room had its own miniature refrigerator, which struck me as a lot more practical than the usual ten-ounce ice buckets that most U.S. hotels stuck you with, which I always assumed was just their way of making sure you patronized room service instead of a nearby grocery store. Now if I could just find a place that sold Cokes or whatever the Australian equivalent was, and maybe a couple of cold cuts, I might actually be able to come out a dollar or two ahead on my expense account.

But as I started to say, the upstairs observer was doing his best to convince me that most of the evening had been at best a hallucination, or at worst something that was none of my business and which was totally beyond my reach and comprehension. And I had to admit that simply ignoring the whole affair and going about my assigned business, once I got a little rest, was by far the easiest alternative. I didn't like even to think what Mike or the wheels back at the *Clarion* would say if they found out I had deviated from the schedule they had so meticulously laid out for me. Besides, the observer pointed out logically, there was always the possibility that there might be danger involved, above and beyond what might happen when Mike got his hands on me.

By the time I was unpacked and had my wrinkled shirts and trousers hung up, I had almost fully convinced myself that I should mind my own business if at all possible, and I might have completed the con job if the phone hadn't rung at the wrong time. It was Kay, of course, and once she started talking and asking questions, I was lost, at least for the rest of the evening, despite the incipient exhaustion I was feeling after being awake, except for short naps, for more than twenty-four hours. There was something about Kay, aside from the obvious physical qualities, and I couldn't help but wonder if her sometimes-when-the-moon-is-just-right talent for, literally, reflecting a person's emotions back at him, usually in amplified form, might not be operating again, even over the phone. But whatever the reason, the curiosity I had more or less beaten into submission staged a sudden recovery at the sound of her voice, and before I fully appreciated what I was doing, I found myself agreeing to meet her in the hotel coffee shop in five minutes.

It took ten, though, to find the place, hidden as it was at the bottom of seemingly endless flights of stairs, at least in the basement and maybe in a subbasement. It didn't look much like a coffee shop, either, but more like a fancy restaurant. There wasn't even a lunch counter, which was my normal habitat while eating. Still, it was a place to sit down, and I slumped gratefully into a chair facing Kay.

As I leaned my elbows on the narrow table between us and rested my face in my hands, I realized that, though it seemed impossible, she looked the same as she had in Los Angeles—wide awake and ready for anything. There was a faint redness in her eyes, presumably from lack of sleep, but that was all. Her voice and curiosity were most certainly not impaired, which is why, after a couple of minutes of halfheartedly avoiding the subject, I ended up telling her about the wavering wombat and the hairy arms. And frankly, it was something of a relief to tell it to someone who believed it. Someone who not only believed it but was fascinated by it.

"A wombat?" Her voice was loud enough to warrant a couple of brief, puzzled glances from a nearby table. "You're sure?"

"Of course I'm sure. There was a picture of one in the *Clarion* a few months ago."

"Of course, your trick memory. Since I don't have one myself, I keep forgetting how handy one is. But this wavering air—was it the same as when Bob's brother vanished last year?"

"More or less, although I didn't see him disappear all that often. But it was just like our oversized friend this evening. Except for the hairy arms and hands."

Kay was looking thoughtful. "I wonder what *this* guy's hands and arms looked like?" she mused. "They were pretty big, and what with the long sleeves and gloves, we couldn't see if they were hairy or not. Did your wombat-removal squad have six fingers, by any chance?"

I shook my head and realized it was beginning to ache a little. "I don't think so," I said, trying to replay the scene in my head. "The light wasn't too great, and those flashbulbs didn't improve my vision much."

"Big, hairy arms . . . Well, there's King Kong and Mighty Joe Young, and maybe Bigfoot. You have any ideas yourself?"

"Bigfoot? As in Yeti and Abominable Snow Men?"

She grinned. "An Abominable Pedestrian, maybe?"

"Sure," I agreed, beginning to feel lightheaded, "that's why no one's ever been able to get a close look at one—they can disappear. And they have pet wombats instead of cats."

Kay laughed. "Or dogs. Your hairy hands were just out walking the wombat. Did you check your desk after the creature disappeared?"

"Not closely, but I think I would've noticed something like that. It was a pretty big wombat. Or maybe it was just foraging. It did eat half an eraser . . ."

I was definitely feeling lightheaded, and for a moment I tried to figure out what time it was back home. Probably four or five in the morning, when I'd normally be asleep and dreaming instead of awake and dreaming.

Then, as I came out of my fruitless mathematical reverie, I saw that Kay was looking past me and waving. Since the only people she knew in Australia were, presumably, the ones who had come over on the plane, I was pretty sure who she was waving to, and when I looked around, I saw that, unfortunately, I was right. Radsack and a herd of a half dozen others, most of whom I recognized from the plane, were flowing around the tables toward us.

There were no introductions, of course, but I remembered a few of names from the plane, and some others popped up as the alleged conversation continued. There was Rusty, with his bushy, red-gray beard, and a dapper little Australian with a neatly trimmed beard and short hair. He was apparently "Eric," and his English was accented but easily understandable. Then there was another American named Denny, who was even taller and thinner than Radsack and who sported a huge mustache and sideburns that had gotten completely out of hand but weren't really a beard. Denny, it seemed, never spoke unless it was to make puns—bad puns, at that. Not that there are any really good ones, but his were particularly atrocious. Even jet lag and lack of sleep couldn't really account for them.

Radsack had apparently been telling them about our encounter, as promised, and from the hurt tone of his voice, it was plain that he couldn't understand why they were all treating it as a great joke. After my experiences last year, I wasn't at all surprised, and I recalled that Kay had said earlier that Radsack was relatively new to science fiction fandom and that this was to be his first convention. I could only assume that he hadn't encountered large groups of fans before. My own brief exposure to the species had taught me quickly that, in groups at least, they tend to consider *everything* a great joke, up to and including dead bodies. Some kind of mob psychology, I suppose, only instead of physically attacking anything in sight, they go after it verbally, looking for laughs instead of blood. The lesser of two evils, but still . . .

"The Beast with Six Fingers," someone in the back of the group said at one point. "Sounds unpleasant."

"Enough to make you Naish your teeth," someone else said, and then added, just to make sure everyone got it, "even if your name isn't J. Carrol."

But you see what I mean. And why Radsack, who was deadly serious about the whole thing, was close to tears and/or apoplexy.

"Now, look, mates," he was almost pleading, "I'm not joking! Just ask Kay! She was— You do still have the bloody disk, don't you, Kay?"

"Right here," she said, patting her purse, "but I don't think it's going to convince anyone, Irv."

"But you got it from—"

"*I* know where I got it, and *you* know where I got it. But its not that spectacular all by itself, you realize."

Radsack blinked, looking as if his last friend in the world had deserted him. "But I thought at least *you* believed it!"

"I do. I'm just warning you, that's all."

"How about it, Kay?" Eric asked. "What went on? You're a levelheaded type."

She shrugged, apparently not wanting to come out foursquare for Radsack for some reason. From the fact that she had talked me into coming down here and confiding in her about the wombat, I knew that she was very definitely interested and pretty definitely convinced it wasn't a hoax. I could only assume that, unlike Radsack, she knew better than to buck the odds without something a lot more convincing than a blank disk to back up her story.

"The disk, the bloody disk!" Radsack was saying, and he looked as if he were about to grab Kay's purse and start digging for the disk himself.

"All right," Kay said, "but don't forget that I—"

Kay stopped in midsentence, a sudden frown creasing her brow. Her eyes darted around the room beyond the cluster of fans.

"What's wrong?" I asked hastily. I remembered the sudden change of expression from last year, and it had always presaged something unpleasant for someone.

"I don't know," she said slowly, nervously. "I . . . felt something. I think."

"More of your emotion dowsing?" I asked quietly, not really

caring to have anyone else hear me, but I needn't have worried. A general hubbub had broken out, and everyone except Radsack and myself were looking around, casting suspicious glances at everyone else in the coffee shop.

"I don't think so," Kay said. "Not unless it's changed recently. And I haven't been picking up much lately anyway. Excitement over the trip blocking things, maybe. But this . . ."

I felt a faint shiver ripple around my back at the way her voice trailed off and her eyes roamed apprehensively around the room.

"What is it, then?" I asked. "Don't tell me you've developed something new."

She only shook her head and frowned, but still her eyes darted about apprehensively, as if she were afraid something was trying to sneak up on her. Then her gaze went downward abruptly, to where her purse sat on the chair next to her like a medium-size shopping bag. Her frown deepened as she reached for the purse and fumbled with the catch, and then began poking in the various pockets and compartments. A moment later, she froze, and I was sure I could see fear in her eyes.

"What—" I began, but before I could say more, her hand emerged from the purse, clamped tightly shut.

Her lips parted, but she didn't speak. Slowly, the babble around us died down until the only sounds were the muted conversations from other tables and the momentary clatter of change being dropped into the cash register several yards away. As the bubble of silence grew, all eyes drifted toward Kay, toward her now-rigid face, and then, one by one, toward her closed fist as she lowered it onto the table.

Then her own eyes, as if reluctant—afraid—to confront what she must already know was there, moved down to the hand. Slowly, palm up, the hand opened.

The disk lay in her palm. Only now it was no longer gray and featureless. Instead, it pulsed with a faint, silvery glow, like the tail of a giant firefly.

"Who is it?"

"There's no need to be so jumpy, Maurtiss. It's just me."

"You didn't use the code knock! I was sure it was him! He's al-

ways nosing around somewhere, and you— I'm having enough trouble without you getting careless and scaring me half to death!"

"I'm sorry, Maurtiss, I just didn't think—"

"That seems to be everyone's problem lately. You didn't think, and now I've got to get this blasted thing tuned in again."

"Tuned in again?"

"Of course! You don't think I would dare have that showing on the screen if you had been Bondeach, do you? And speaking of the devil, where is our beloved inspector?"

"Looking over some organization charts, I think."

"Good, good, that will keep him out of our hair for a while. Ah, here we go. How does that look? In focus pretty well?"

"Excellent. How is it going?"

"I'm not sure yet. At least Artil's got a larger audience this time, although . . . Let me ask you, Verrmond, have you ever had any personal contact with the natives?"

"Me, sir? Hardly. I'm sure I couldn't pass, and I'm just as happy that way. That little charade this evening was quite enough contact to last me until my term is up."

"Which may be sooner than you expect, Verrmond, if you don't keep your codes straight . . ."

VI

"You Couldn't Fool Blind Freddy with a Line Like That"

As if someone had lifted the covers off a dozen parrot cages, everyone in the cluster began talking at once. Those at the other tables probably turned to see what caused the sudden outbursts, but I didn't notice. I was still staring at the pulsing, silvery disk in Kay's palm, wondering if it was really growing brighter with each pulse or if it was my imagination.

Finally, one of the voices broke out of the general scramble of sound. It was Radsack's, and it had a decidedly triumphant note in it:

"*That's* the disk I was telling you about!"

"You didn't say it glowed," someone in the group said.

"It didn't, not then. I don't know why—"

"Interesting, I admit, but hardly conclusive proof of the existence of extraterrestrials." It was a smooth voice, not particularly loud, but somehow it overwhelmed the others, sort of like a velvet-lined steam roller. "It appears to me to be merely a relaxation oscillator."

I looked up to find that Denver Cross had not only joined the group but had managed to slither to the front, next to the table. He was eying the pulsing disk with an amusedly superior air.

Radsack turned to stare blankly at Denver, and it seemed to take a moment for him to recover from the interruption.

"*What*," Radsack finally asked, "is a bloody relaxation oscillator?"

"Oh, I'm sure you've seen one." The calm, lecturing tone drowned out the babble around us, and gradually the sounds died away as the babblers searched for the source and finally centered on Denver. "Novelty companies sold them by the millions. Why I never patented my own— But that is neither here nor there. Usually the devices were concealed in a small box, with three or more bulbs protruding from one side."

"Yeah, I remember," Rusty agreed. "They'd just sit there, flashing on and off in no order whatsoever, over and over, until it drove you crazy or you stuck it in a drawer."

"And even then, you *knew* they were there, blinking happily away . . ." Eric said. "They even had them over here."

Rusty was shaking his shaggy head. "I can see why you'd call them oscillators, but why relaxation? They sure never relaxed me."

Denver nodded sagely. "Merely a reference to the circuitry involved. If you wish, I could diagram the pertinent elements, but . . ." He looked at the pulsing disk, then picked it up from the table top where Kay had laid it a few seconds before.

"This one has apparently been molded inside a plastic disk," he said as he turned the disk slowly in his hands, peering at it closely. The pulsing light cast odd, greenish shadows on his face as he spoke. "Excellent workmanship for what is essentially a toy, really excellent. I do wonder who the manufacturer is. Most mass-produced products today are inexcusably shabby, really deplorable. Even the company with which I am associated has its problems, though I certainly do what I can."

"I'd heard America was coming apart at the joints," an obviously Australian voice said.

"It is hardly a uniquely American problem," Denver returned. "Europeans, for instance, are often awed by the so-called 'German efficiency,' but I happen to know that Volkswagen is looking for a factory site in the United States. They hope, of course, to achieve lower costs in the long run, and get better quality work. This won't be general knowledge for another few months, you realize, but I was talking to a member of the Bundestag not long ago—"

Radsack, who had been spluttering behind his beard, finally got some words out, loudly and plaintively. "But there aren't any bulbs in this thing! And the whole thing is glowing!"

"Translucent plastic, of course," Denver informed him mildly, "or perhaps one of the new, electroluminescent materials, although that would seem a trifle expensive for a toy such as this." Casually, he laid the disk back on the table.

"Look," Radsack said, plowing into the momentary silence, "the logical thing to do is to take this to someone who really knows electronics. That way we can be sure what it is."

This touched off another hubbub, and from the few coherent phrases I caught, the majority were quite satisfied with Denver's explanation and felt they had better things to do than run around Sydney shopping for an electronics expert.

"Before we do anything else, how about trying to turn it off?" It was Kay. She had picked up the disk again and was examining it the way Denver had been. "I can't find any switch or button or anything, and frankly it's starting to get on my nerves, whatever it is."

"Most unlikely that there is a switch," Denver said. "I myself saw no controls, and I rather imagine there are none to be found. These devices normally are simply allowed to run continuously until the battery is depleted."

"But it wasn't glowing before," Radsack objected. "It must have been turned on somehow!"

Denver shrugged, as if the matter was so obvious that it was hardly worth the effort to explain. "One can do marvelous things with timing circuits," he said.

"How long before the battery runs down?" someone wondered.

"Who knows?" It was Rusty again, holding his arm up to display a wristwatch. "This thing runs a year on a battery half the size of a dime, so—"

"A faulty analogy," Denver interpolated. "The energy required to produce this light is considerably greater than what is required to run a watch. You must remember, in pocket calculators, for instance—the field in which I am currently involved—the vast majority of the energy is used to illuminate the display, not perform the calculations."

"Batteries? Calculators?" Radsack exploded again. "What's the *matter* with you people? You're worrying about these bloody details, when— Did you all forget where this thing *came* from?"

"I thought it came from her purse," Rusty said, grinning at Kay.

"You bloody well know what I mean!" Radsack looked apoplectic, but, strangely, his accent seemed even less thick than the last time I'd thought about it. I couldn't help but think of the old joke about people with British accents:

"Wake one of them up suddenly in the middle of the night and he'll talk just like anyone else."

"Sure, I know what you mean," Rusty said. "You got it from some guy in the street, and—"

"Some guy in the street?" Radsack almost screamed. "Some guy? A bloody giant, he was, and he disappeared right before our eyes!"

"He didn't vanish right before my eyes," Rusty said.

"It would've been before your eyes if you'd been there! My god, what do you want? We all saw it—Don and Kay and that little bloke, Adams, and—and—" He broke off, pointing at me.

Rusty, who seemed to have become a spokesman of sorts for the group, shrugged. "So? I know a bunch of people who swear a Hieronymous Machine works for them, or who say they've located underground water with a bent coat hanger. I even know one guy who says he has personally seen a UFO, and somebody else who got a message from God."

"And you think they're all liars?" Radsack inquired hotly.

"I didn't say that. Some of them may believe what they say, for all I know. But that doesn't mean I have to believe any of it myself."

The general background hubbub was picking up again, and Radsack stood looking at the lot of them, his mouth slightly ajar behind the thick beard. Finally, he shook his head and said, plaintively, "Don't you believe in *anything*? You're as bad as Thompson!"

"Don? Oh yes, your other witness," Rusty said. "That brings up another point. If all this happened right in front of Don's eyes, why didn't *he* say something about it? I saw him just a few minutes ago, and—"

"How should I know?" Radsack flailed his long arms like an out-of-synch windmill, and I noticed one of the waitresses a few tables away eying him suspiciously—even more suspiciously than she was eying the rest of the group.

"Look," Radsack went on, gesturing at the disk, which was still pulsing steadily, "do you want to find out what this thing is or not?"

Kay reached out and snatched up the disk. "I don't know about anyone else," she said firmly, "but *I* would like to find out."

"Bloody tremendous!" Radsack said, then glanced at the others. "Anyone else? Or is Kay the only sane and curious person in this whole bloody crowd? I thought that of all people, science fiction readers would be open-minded enough to—"

He stopped as several chuckles erupted from the group, and a loud "Ahah!" came from Rusty, who was looking knowingly at Radsack.

"How long have you been in fandom, anyway?" Rusty asked.

Radsack blinked, clearly taken aback at the sudden and irrelevant question. "Not long," he said finally, "but what does that—"

"You ever hear of the Shaver Mystery? Or Dianetics?" Rusty persisted.

Radsack's face shifted from total confusion to tentative confidence. "Of course I have."

"All right," Rusty said, "what were they?"

"What is this, a quiz?"

"Something like that. Just tell us, what do you think they were?"

Radsack shrugged his bony shoulders. "All right, if you insist, and if it will get you people moving. Somebody named Richard Shaver wrote a series of stories for . . . *Amazing Stories*, wasn't it? Anyway, it was back in the forties, and Shaver claimed they were fact, not fiction." Despite the relatively informal language, the words struck me as being something he was reciting from memory, although the accent and its varying thickness made it hard to be sure.

"I never saw any of them myself," Radsack was going on, "but I understand he claimed there were some sort of creatures—deros?—still living in caverns in the Earth. Survivors of some civilization that had destroyed itself, or maybe been destroyed by something else, I forget which. Like I said, I never read the things myself. But these creatures, whatever they were, were supposed to have some machines left over from that other civilization, and they could use them to zap humans on the surface. Isn't that about it?"

Rusty laughed. "Close enough. And Dianetics?"

Radsack frowned again. "I don't really see— Oh, all right. Dianetics? That was a little later, I think. Started out as a sort of super-quickie psychoanalysis, but it eventually turned into a religion of sorts."

"Of sorts, right," Rusty said. "And it made the 'founder'—who used to be a fair to middling sf writer himself—into a million-aire."

"So? What does all this have to do with anything? What's the bloody point?"

"The point is, practically no one in fandom ever believed a word of either of those things."

"You . . . didn't?" What little of Radsack's face was visible behind the beard seemed paler. "But I thought—"

"I repeat, ahah!" Rusty said, wagging a finger in Radsack's general direction. "You are suffering from the same delusions that the mundanes—led around by their mental noses by the media types—suffer from." His eyes had given me a brief bruis-ing as he mentioned media types. "You think that just because we read about all kinds of 'weird things,' we'll believe anything that comes along?"

"But the circulation of that magazine when Shaver was—"

"Mundanes, not fans," Rusty said. "The same ones that are making Von Däniken and Berlitz and their ilk rich these days. We'll take deCamp or Kusche over those phonies any day."

"Kusche?" Radsack was looking blanker by the second. "I've heard of deCamp, of course, but—"

"A research librarian," Rusty explained. "He's got a book com-ing out that really shows up all those Bermuda Triangle odd-balls. Explains almost all the so-called 'disappearances' and shows where Berlitz and all the rest got their alleged information —which was usually a story by some reporter who was too lazy to check his facts," he added, glancing at me again.

"But I just read a story," Radsack protested, "just a couple of weeks ago, about the Bermuda Triangle, and it—"

"A *story*, friend, a *story!* Fiction, not fact. Sf says, 'What if it *was* like this? What would happen then?' The UFO and Bermuda Triangle and occult folk say, 'Hey, people, this is what it's really like.' You see the distinction?"

"Another distinction," Eric put in, a bit gloomily, "is that *they* are the ones that make all the money."

Radsack glanced around the group again, as if looking for support, but he found none. Then his eyes slid back to the disk, still laying on the table, still pulsing silently, as it had throughout Rusty's entire educational lecture.

"All right," Radsack said, giving the impression of someone who was trying to drag himself out of a pit of verbal quicksand, "never mind all that other stuff. Just look at this." He pointed at the disk. "*Something* happened this evening, and a couple of us—" He darted a look at Kay. "A couple of us bloody well want to find out what it was. Now if any of the rest of you are interested . . . ?"

Rusty and a couple of the others shrugged. "I never said we weren't interested," he said, "or curious. Now as I recall, before we were all sidetracked, you were saying something about a friendly, neighborhood electronics expert?"

Radsack blinked at the sudden apparent reversal in Rusty's attitude. "That's right, but I thought—"

"All right, then," Rusty said, "perhaps we should all adjourn until morning, and then, if the portable pulsar here hasn't itself vanished, we can consult an expert."

Radsack was looking a little better now, although he still seemed a bit unsure of himself. "Why not right now?" he asked.

"You know where to find an expert at this time of night?" Rusty looked at Radsack suspiciously.

"It's a friend of mine," Radsack said. "He lives just a few blocks from here, in Paddington." He hesitated at the looks of skepticism he was getting from most of the group. "And what he doesn't know about electronics isn't worth knowing," he added, a touch of defiance in his voice.

"If he's that good," Eric remarked, "what's he doing in Paddington? It's not what you'd call the ideal location, unless he's selling burglar alarms."

Radsack shrugged, more of his confidence returning. "It's not all that bad any more, not since the artist types started moving in. Besides, he likes it there." He glanced around at the group again. "Now, are we going or not?"

Kay took the lead by grasping the disk and standing up. The pulsing, I noticed, seemed dimmer now. "Let's go," she said, then looked back at me. "You coming, Joe?"

Being a mild-mannered reporter—or travel writer at the moment—I tend to listen more than talk, especially when I don't have anything to say, so I just nodded and got up to follow her. There are times when I remind myself of Charlie Brown. I was as curious as anyone else, but I still wasn't enthusiastic. In fact, I was a little worried. If my so-called serendipity was still working —and the goings-on of the last few hours pretty much confirmed that it was—who knows what we would run into while wandering the streets of night-time Sydney? What we had already run into was more than enough for my taste.

In the end, everyone went on the expedition except Denver, who said he had an early appointment with some important city officials and needed some rest. Aside from Kay and Radsack and myself, though, no one openly admitted he was going because he really believed the disk was anything particularly mysterious or that the alleged six-fingered disappearing giant was necessarily real. They all found reasons to trail along, though.

"I always like to look over new cities, especially at night."

"After twenty hours on that plane, I need a little exercise."

"Maybe we'll spot some bookstores we can visit tomorrow."

At least the misty rain that had been falling earlier had stopped by the time we all emerged into the street, and the glare of the headlights and neon signs up and down the length of Williams Street made the expedition seem less unnerving. It was like being in the middle of any large U.S. city. There was even a huge, flashing Coca-Cola sign on a nearby rooftop to make us feel at home. Around the corner from Williams, though, things turned darker and dingier, and what someone had said earlier, about the hotel being in the middle of the Australian version of Greenwich Village combined with a red light district, came back to me. The lights were fewer and farther between, and all kinds of shops, mostly closed, lined the streets, along with tiny restaurants and scroungy-looking night clubs, and a fair number of potentially friendly—for a fee—girls. The few pedestrians we passed seemed furtive, but maybe it was just us. Running into a group like ours—large, noisy, and with clothes ranging from conservative business suits to ragged blue jeans and stockmen's boots—was enough to make anyone furtive until he was out of range.

Paddington, despite Radsack's repeated assurances, turned out to be farther than anyone really wanted to go, but by the time anyone realized this, we were past the point of no return. Even so, there were a few defections. A couple dropped out when we passed a particularly appetizing bookstore window, and another walker, young and male, dropped out when something else apparently looked particularly appetizing to him. Radsack was appalled by the defections, but there was nothing he could do about them.

Meanwhile, there had been another dropout of sorts: The disk. The apparent dimming I had noticed back in the coffee shop had turned out to be real as well as progressive, and by the time we were two blocks from the hotel, it had died altogether. After the disk was quickly passed around and again examined unsuccessfully for hidden controls, it was dropped into Kay's purse.

Then, on a particularly dreary-looking block with one street lamp burned out, Kay suddenly stopped. The rest of us stumbled to a lumpy halt around her.

"What now?" Rusty asked.

Kay shook her head and snapped open her purse. It didn't take long to find the disk. The entire interior of the purse was filled with a greenish-silver glow, and this time it was almost steady, though I could still see a periodic variation. It was brighter, too, by quite a bit, as bright as a strong flashlight, except that this was a soft light, even softer than a fluorescent tube.

For a change, everyone was silent as Kay brought the disk out into the open and let it cast eerie shadows in all directions. Kay, I could see, was shivering. I reached out and put a hand on her arm, and she moved toward me just a fraction.

The silence was broken by a voice from somewhere in the group: "If there's an honest man in the crowd, how about stepping forward? Maybe then that thing will go out for good."

There were a few chuckles, but all were touched with nervousness. Being cool and disbelieving in a well-lighted coffee shop was one thing; on a dimly lighted, deserted, unfamiliar street, it was something else altogether, and I got the feeling that Radsack realized this, because before anyone else had a chance to say anything, he grabbed Kay's other arm and said loudly:

"Come on. Gary only lives around the corner from here. Maybe we can get there while this thing is still operating. At least it'll give him a firsthand idea of what it does."

Kay hesitated a moment, holding back, but then she began to move with him. At first it was a fast walk, but after a dozen yards, Radsack broke into a trot. I hurried after them, while the rest of the group ambled along behind us in a milling cluster. Various mumbles were breaking out, including something obscure about "fleet messengers of Ahura Mazda," as the three of us in the lead turned the corner.

Kay and Radsack were a couple of yards ahead of me, and we were all maybe a dozen yards past the corner when things started happening. First, a blob of air a few feet in front of us started wavering. Kay and Radsack were both watching the glowing disk in Kay's hand, so neither of them seemed to see the wavering.

I yelled, something unspecific and not too helpful, like "Look out!" Kay started to look around toward me, not ahead toward the wavering air, and Radsack didn't do anything but continue to plow ahead.

I tried to lunge forward and grab them—or at least grab Kay —but it didn't quite work out. I lunged, all right, but I also slipped on something, probably because I was watching the wavering air, which now filled an area at least seven feet high and a yard wide, rather than watching where my feet were going.

Anyway, in midlunge, I thumped into Radsack's bony back and sent him flying forward at an angle in front of Kay, who had skidded to a full stop and was turning toward me. Radsack, though light, had been weighty enough to enable me to regain my balance in a lurching fashion, and I managed to come to a halt.

Radsack, too, managed to stop, but not before he was practically in contact with the patch of wavering air. I heard him gasp. A moment later, he, too, was wavering, just like the air, and frantically trying to backpedal. Before he could make any progress, though, a pair of disembodied arms appeared. Hairy arms, just like the ones that had grabbed the wombat. The hairy arms grabbed Radsack very firmly by the shoulders.

And Radsack disappeared, just like the wombat.

But not the wavering air. That remained.

And as I watched, I began to see patterns in the wavering air. There was more than the simple distortion of things seen through the wavering area, and what I had to do was try to ignore the images, ignore the pastel-painted row houses and the half dozen cars, parked and empty. I couldn't do it completely, of course, but I did manage in a limited fashion, and as I did, other shapes emerged, shapes formed by the wavering itself, phantom shapes that moved and shifted and twisted in the air itself.

Like the ones that had moved and shifted and twisted in the blackness of the doorway from which the six-fingered giant had emerged . . .

It was about then that I noticed for the first time the same not-quite-sixty-cycle hum that had poured out of that same door, but now it wasn't nearly as loud.

I felt Kay's hand on my arm then, either grasping it for support—unlikely—or urging me to back up, which was something I should have thought of myself. It would be nice to say that I was analyzing the situation, considering the odds against rescuing Radsack from whatever limbo he had disappeared into, but I wasn't doing anything remotely like that. I was just standing there, recording everything like the eidetic idiot I am, not a single thought, constructive or otherwise, running through my head. If my breathing hadn't been on automatic, I suspect I would've neglected that, too.

Abruptly, one of the wavering shapes solidified. It was Radsack, his feet dangling about four inches above the sidewalk.

For one insane instant, the hairy hands and arms were there, too, clutching Radsack's bony shoulders, but then they were gone, and Radsack clattered to the ground, stumbling backward as he hit, but not quite falling over.

Then the wavering was gone, as well as the subdued hum.

And the disk, still clutched in Kay's fist, stopped glowing.

A second later, Rusty and the rest of the cluster rounded the corner. The timing was perfect.

Radsack seemed to have regained his balance by then, but he was looking around wildly in all directions. I could hear him muttering something, but it was either too soft or too accented for me to make out.

"What's going on now?" Rusty inquired as the group strolled up. "Is this where your chum hangs out?"

Radsack spun around to face them, but it was Kay who spoke: "This time *Irv* vanished!"

"He did?" Rusty looked at her puzzledly. "Then who's that?" he asked, pointing at Radsack.

She sighed in exasperation. "He reappeared."

Another general hubbub, like what had been going on back in the hotel, erupted. "How about that?" Rusty said, apparently in good spirits again. "Very fast work there, Irv. You disappear and then reappear, all between the time you got around the corner and the time we did. Must have come and gone, or vice versa, in a literal flash." He shook his head. "The least you could've done was wait for us to show up."

"It wasn't *my* ideal" Radsack said nervously, the first intelligible words he had uttered since his reappearance. "But they— *You* saw it!" He looked pleadingly at Kay and me. "Didn't you?"

Rusty laughed, turning to the tall, thin girl next to him. "Does all this remind you of something? Like perhaps an old Abbott and Costello movie? Lou never *could* get anything to happen when anyone else was in the room, and—"

The girl was looking blank. "Abbott and Costello?"

Rusty sighed. "You make me feel my years. They were the slapstick Smothers Brothers of my generation."

"Oh," the girl said, "them. I think I saw them once, in a classic movie series on campus."

Rusty rolled his eyes in despair. "At any rate," he said, "I have the distinct impression that I've seen this scene before, and it was better acted the first time."

Radsack, his eyes darting back and forth following the dialogue, was getting twitchier by the second. Abruptly, without audibly sighing, he seemed to shrink slightly, and he turned his attention to Kay.

"Come on," Radsack said hurriedly, "let's get to Gary's place before those things pop up again. It's just down the block."

Without waiting, he pulled away from us and started down the sidewalk at a rapid, gangling pace. Kay and I, after only a moment's hesitation, followed at a slightly faster clip. The others milled around for a few seconds and began a sort of Brownian movement in our direction.

"Come on, Irv, *what happened?*" Kay demanded as she caught up with Radsack.

"I wish I knew," he said, without slackening his pace, speaking as rapidly as he was walking. "All I know is, after you"—he glared at me accusingly—"after you slammed into me, everything around me started to—well, everything was out of focus, I guess. And then something grabbed me. I'll bet I've got the bruises to prove it, too, if those—"

He glanced over his shoulder toward the trailing cluster but kept moving.

"Never mind the bruises," Kay persisted. "You were grabbed. And then what happened? Did you see what was on the other end of the arms?"

"It was too dark to see much, darker than the street here. Looked like I was inside a building, and I think I saw walls. As for what grabbed me—they looked sort of human."

"They? There was more than one?"

His stride faltered for a step, and he resumed. "A couple of them, I think. They weren't as big as those arms would make you think. And the faces were covered with hair. Or covered with *something* dark."

"But where *were* you? Couldn't you tell at all? Nothing but walls?"

"I told you, it was pretty dark. Might've been a machine of some sort, but—"

"What kind of machine?"

Another falter in his stride. "How should *I* know? It didn't have a label saying 'radio' or 'computer,' or if it did, I couldn't see it. It was just a machine, about five feet high with a bunch of knobs and things. Then—"

Radsack stopped speaking and almost stopped walking, and his expression brightened.

"And they said something," he said, his voice cheering up along with his face. "Something like, 'It's the wrong one!'"

"In English?" Kay sounded more surprised by this than by anything else.

"Definitely," he said, sounding pleased with himself.

Before Kay could ask more, Radsack stopped abruptly at the foot of one of the sets of steps that led up to the front of the row houses. They looked vaguely like New York brownstones, except that none of them were brown. Most were light blue or green or even yellow, although it was hard to tell precise colors in the dim light. The one we were in front of, though, was unmistakably pink.

After only a brief hesitation, Radsack hurried up the steps and knocked on the door, glancing back toward Kay and me as he did. It couldn't have been more than a second before the door swung open, and I wondered if we had been expected, or if the occupant spent all his time within a yard of the front door. The young man—Gary, I assumed—who opened the door was tall, gangling, and slightly stooped. He could have been Radsack's clean-shaven brother.

"Irv?" The young man looked surprised. "What brings you here, mate? I fancied you were having a go at some sort of convention."

"I will be, but not for a day or two. Look, mate, can we come in?" Radsack glanced around nervously, not at Kay or me or at the cluster of fans who were ambling within earshot at the moment, but at everything else—the empty street, the sidewalk, the buildings, even the sky, as if he were expecting it to open up and grab him again, for which I couldn't really blame him.

Gary looked toward Kay and me at the bottom of the short flight of steps. "Of course," he said. "Are these some of your chums from the convention?"

Radsack nodded hastily. "I'll explain in a minute. Right now I—"

"Of course, of course. Do come in." Gary smiled down at us as he stood back and held the door open.

"The others, too," Radsack said, indicating the ambling half dozen, now only a few yards away.

Gary looked a bit dubious. "All of them?"

"Sure, all of them. Now come on, mate, can we—"

"Fair enough," Gary said, apparently acquiescing with good grace.

Radsack stood at the top of the steps, waving everyone inside and going through a series of perfunctory introductions as we all trooped past, telling everyone this was his friend Gary. He missed a few of the names in the cluster, including mine.

Inside, the apartment didn't look that much different from a typical U.S. low or middle income apartment, though it was a bit more colorful. There were the standard chairs and tables and sofas and an ancient-looking console TV in one corner. The only oddity was what I first thought was an abstract painting but which turned out, on closer inspection, to be a multi-colored circuit diagram, which I thought was perhaps a bit much for someone who had been billed as an electronics expert.

Once everyone was milling around in the living room, Gary turned his attention to Radsack. "All right, mate, you want to give me the drum?"

Radsack looked puzzled for a moment, then brightened. "Oh, of course. We've run into something a bit awkward in the electronics line. Thought you might take a look—take a screw at it."

Gary hesitated, glancing around at the crowd, then shrugged. "I can give it a burl, sure. What is it?"

Radsack turned to Kay. "The disk?" He sounded like an uncertain surgeon asking for a scalpel.

Obediently, she opened her fist and held the disk out to him. "It quit working again," she explained.

Radsack took the disk and held it out to Gary.

Until then, Gary had been smiling, a bit uncertainly, probably wondering what was going on. Now, as he saw the disk for the first time, the smile froze, then shattered. He even seemed to shrink back, although he didn't actually take a step backward.

"You ever see anything like this before?" Radsack asked, apparently not noticing Gary's reaction. "It's not doing it now, but every so often it glows. I don't know if it— Does it get warm then, Kay?" he asked, turning toward her.

Kay shook her head silently. She was watching Gary puzzledly.

"Where did you get that?" Gary's voice was a whisper, but it was so intense that he was suddenly the center of attention.

"It's a long story, mate," Radsack said. "I'll give you the whole thing over a bottle of stout if you want, but right now we just want to know what it is. Since you—"

"No," Gary said sharply, shaking his head. "I don't know what it is. I don't have any idea!"

"But you haven't even looked at it!" Radsack protested. "Come on, you said you'd give it a burl. The trouble is, sometimes it glows, but now—"

Gary shook his head again, still refusing to take the disk in his hand. "I have no idea what it could be. Anyway, all my equipment is at the shop. I couldn't— You say it glows?" The question was hesitant, uncertain. "When does it . . . glow?"

"Just a few minutes ago, as a matter of fact," Radsack said.

Gary's eyes widened. "Where? Not near here?"

"Of course, near here. Just down the block, as a matter of fact. But I don't see what—"

Gary's mouth snapped shut, and his eyes blinked rapidly for a moment. "I'm sorry," he said abruptly, "but I don't have any idea what that thing might be. And I really don't have the time right now. I really must—"

"What?" Radsack frowned. "You haven't even touched it! And you told me—"

"I've seen quite enough. There's nothing I can tell you." Gary's voice was brittle, the words rapid, almost stumbling over each other.

"Here, now," Radsack said, still frowning, "don't drop your bundle! All we want to know is—"

"I'm sorry. I can't help you. Now please, I must— Some galah wants me to check his alarm system yet tonight, and I have to get ready. You must excuse me."

Futilely, he was trying to herd the entire group back into the hall and out the door.

"Stiffen the lizards, mate!" Radsack protested as Gary tried to grasp his arm and urge him on. "Don't go lemony on me! I don't want to be a bloody standover merchant, but you couldn't fool Blind Freddy with a line like that! You *do* know something, don't you?" Radsack held out the disk toward Gary, who jerked back reflexively.

"No! I don't—" He turned nervous, pleading eyes on Kay. "Miss—Miss Clarke? Get rid of it!" he said urgently. "Throw it away! Destroy it! Do whatever you bloody well want, but get rid of it!"

His eyes slipped again toward the disk in Radsack's hand, and he moved back nervously. "Now go! Please, all of you!"

Kay reached out and took the disk from Radsack's unresisting grip. "That's all right," she said, "we're going."

"No," Radsack said sharply. "He knows something, and—"

By now the entire group, following Kay's lead, was milling in the general direction of the door, and Gary had rushed ahead and thrown it open. In a minute, despite Radsack's incoherent protests, they were all outside, the door slamming solidly behind them.

The tall, thin girl next to Rusty giggled. "It's not your stone age version of the Smothers Brothers after all," she said. "It's *Invasion from Planet Z.*"

"Are you sure?" someone else asked. "We've been invaded from Hollywood so often, I've lost track. But one thing for sure, I've seen that scene before."

"But this was better acted, maybe even better than that street scene a couple of hours ago," Rusty said, turning toward Radsack. "You and your friends have a great future in the drama, Irv."

Someone else, Denny, I think, applauded loudly but said nothing, probably because he couldn't think of a pun. Radsack looked around angrily, then turned on Rusty.

"Listen, sport," Radsack almost shouted, "couldn't you see that Gary was really dropping his bundle? He was so scared—"

Eric, the only other Australian in the group, was eying Radsack oddly but saying nothing. Again, it was Rusty who interrupted.

"Very dramatic, I'm sure, but overdone a trifle, wouldn't you say, Eric?"

"Chewing the furniture," Eric agreed. "It would've been more effective with a bit less yelling and cringing."

Radsack started to protest again, loudly, but after a couple of syllables, he stopped. His shoulders slumped.

"All right," he said, "if that's the way it is." He shook his head despondently. "We might as well go. I'll call Gary tomorrow myself. Maybe he will have calmed down by then."

And so we began the trek back to the hotel. As before, Kay and Radsack and I were in the lead while the others ambled along behind us. The last I saw or heard of them, they were still busily calling out names and describing plots of movies or TV shows that Gary's performance had reminded them of.

As for me, I wasn't sure what to think. Not that that's unusual. As I've said often enough before, I'm slow to come to decisions, mainly because I've found that if I simply drift along, eventually I'll stumble across something that will make up my mind for me. And things have always "worked out," one way or another, without benefit of any particularly decisive actions on my part. Even my so-called "rescue" of Kay from that teleporting killer last year had been sheer luck—or maybe extrasensory serendipity or even well-disguised telepathy, if I could believe any of Kay's spontaneously combustible theories about me.

In any event, I was coasting as usual, not sure which way to lean. I'd seen our six-finger friend disappear, and I'd been pretty close to Radsack when he'd vanished and reappeared. Maybe I didn't have as much experience covering magician's stage shows as Don did, but I'd seen enough to know that what we'd seen was a long way from simple stage disappearances, Anthony Blake to the contrary. Magicians make people vanish from boxes, not open stages, so it was reasonably obvious that, unless the Australians were extraordinarily gifted along magical or ESP lines, they were not staging all this for the benefit of Kay and Rusty and the rest of the U.S. fans.

On the other hand, I knew that Rusty and the rest were right in pointing out the similarities to various second- and third-rate movies and TV shows. It was all too pat, from the alien who had time to gasp out a lot of cryptic words, to the expert who was too frightened to explain what he was frightened about. Even I had seen those situations a dozen times, and I'm not that much of a movie fan—not that type of movie, anyway. Even taking my so-called serendipity into account, it was a bit on the unreal side. Being on the spot when odd things happen is one thing, but being on the spot when these particular things happen is something else. They shouldn't really be happening at all, anywhere. Still, it wasn't that much weirder than what I'd fallen into last year, which shouldn't have happened anywhere or anytime either . . .

And so it went, wishy-washing back and forth all the way to the hotel. In the end, all I could decide for sure was that *something* was going on and that I didn't understand it. And that tomorrow I had to gather enough material for at least three travel articles, alien invasion or no alien invasion . . .

"All right, Artil, what went wrong this time?"

"It's certainly not my fault he bumped into me! It was those blasted techs that fouled up the works, grabbing me like that without even looking! And then shutting down before I had a chance to get things going again!"

"Don't try to shift the blame to them. They had their instructions, and they followed them the best they could under the circumstances."

"But the circumstances changed! They should have—"

"That was hardly their fault, now was it? These people are your responsibility, Artil, and don't forget it. And while that subject has come up again, I might mention that I was listening in just before that fiasco. Perhaps you might like to explain?"

"Explain? I don't believe I understand."

"You said you had picked this lot because they were likely to believe almost anything. It strikes me that you made a particularly bad selection."

"But a couple of them—"

"A couple out of nearly a dozen is hardly a good average! And even they did not seem overwhelmed by the evidence. Certainly not overwhelmed enough to even willingly tell their friends about it. And from what they were all saying—Artil, let me ask you: Were they right? Did you get these little scenes from some of their mass media entertainments?"

"Well, in a way, sir, but there were enough variations that—"

"*You admit it, then? Why, for God's sake? Why? Didn't you realize they would recognize them?*"

"*But it seemed logical to— I mean, since they were accustomed to this sort of thing, it seemed advisable to give them something similar, something they were familiar with. How was I to know they had this peculiar mind-set? After all—*"

"*You're supposed to have researched them, you nit! And that's another thing—that language you two were throwing at each other. What was that, anyway?*"

"*Just some local slang, sir. I mean, you did comment about it recently, sir, implying that I should—*"

"*Very well, but . . . Are you sure you're using it correctly?*"

"*Of course, sir. I realize it's not on the tapes yet, but if you would like to see the book we obtained it from—*"

"*Never mind. We don't have that much time. Just watch it, that's all, and don't overdo it. Just remember, you're not used to dealing with these people directly. And perhaps you had better start concentrating on just two or three of that lot. Larger groups appear to be counterproductive.*"

"*It may be just this particular group, sir. A subgroup, so to speak. If we can gather together a large enough cross section tomorrow, we're sure to—*"

"*All right, Artil, gather your cross section. But in the meantime, concentrate on the two or three who aren't openly ridiculing you.*"

"*Yes, sir. But the one isn't even a member of—*"

"*Never mind what he is or isn't a member of. He's there and he doesn't seem totally unconvinced. If I were you, I would take advantage of whatever straws I could grasp . . .*"

VII

"They Looked at Me Like I Was a Ratbag"

The next day, I tried to forget the night before while I did my tourist bit. I recorded enough facts and impressions and one-liners to fill up at least the required number of articles. There would be one on the Sydney Opera House, of course, another one or two on the zoo and its denizens (including a wombat, which didn't look nearly as big in a cage as it had on my desk), and even one on the quaint daytime activities of the neighborhood around the hotel. And finally I was thinking about a short piece on the fabulous Sydney Harbour Bridge and the even more fabulous traffic jams that clog it worse than an L.A. freeway. I only wish I had been able to do my research some other way. Sitting motionless in the middle of the bridge for a half hour in my cheapie rented car, courting asphyxiation from exhaust fumes, was something I could've done without. I rather suspect that either Werner or Mike could have warned me about that particular hazard, but, then, neither of them is known for having charitable instincts, especially when they might interfere with a story. I remember, for instance, when a writer called in one morning to say he'd be late because he'd just totaled his car by rolling it over on the expressway, and Mike's first reaction was:

"What were you thinking about while you were rolling over? Think you might be able to get a story out of it?"

All in all, though, it wasn't a bad day, considering that I was being paid for it. The people at the opera house were, for the most part, getting hypersensitive and defensive about bad acoustics and impossible construction costs, not to mention all the toy-sailboat jokes, none of which I had made, luckily, so that was sort of fun. And the koalas and bandicoots and platypuses and all the other weirdly named and shaped animals were cuter than what you would find in your average American zoo, so that wasn't bad, either. The only thing I could really have done without was that wheezing half hour on the bridge.

When I got back to the hotel, though, things deteriorated rapidly. Or picked up rapidly, depending on your point of view.

It started when the elevator opened on the fifth floor for no apparent reason other than my alleged serendipity. I had pushed "eight," which is my floor, and there was no one else in the elevator that I could see and no one was waiting in the fifth-floor corridor when the doors slid open.

There was, however, someone shouting, almost screaming, in the distance, somewhere out of sight around the corner in one of the intersecting corridors. As always, my rational half—my seemingly detached and usually unflappable upstairs observer—suggested calmly that I punch the "CLOSE DOOR" button and try to forget the whole thing. The other half, the impulsive half that didn't think or decide but simply reacted, disagreed, and I was charging out of the elevator before a good internal argument could get underway.

In the dozen yards to the intersecting corridor, however, there was time for a tiny bit of sober reflection and a couple of realizations. First, it was Kay's voice doing the shouting, and second, whatever was going on, it was undoubtedly a continuation of the same insanity we'd fallen into the night before. The two realizations more or less canceled each other out as far as inspiration to action goes. I certainly didn't want to leave Kay in the lurch, whatever that lurch might be, but I didn't really want to get involved with any more disappearing giants or invading aliens. So, after a second or so of stumbling hesitation, I skidded to a halt just short of the intersecting corridor and peered cautiously around the corner.

It was worse than I expected. The wavery spot was there, of course, just like it had been last night in the street. Now it was hanging in midair about twenty feet down the hall. Beyond the spot was what I assumed must have come out of it. There were two of them, both with their backs to me. They were about five and a half feet tall and looked vaguely like skinny gorillas dressed in silvery boots and loose-fitting silvery-gray coveralls with broad belts around the middle. Here, I realized, must be the bodies that went with those disembodied hairy arms.

To make matters worse, the two apes were advancing slowly and methodically toward Kay, Don Thompson, and Radsack, all of whom were trapped at the far end of the short corridor. Kay was holding her enormous purse by the shoulder strap and whirling it over her head and in front of her like a medieval knight with a morning star. Don, on the other hand, simply looked terrified and was trying to back through the wall next to the window. Radsack was darting glances in all directions, looking terribly confused.

Unfortunately, I was just as confused as Radsack seemed to be. I didn't have any idea what the gorillas were up to, although I was sure I wouldn't like it, whatever it was. More to the point, I didn't have any idea what I could do about the situation. Kay, though, apparently had ideas on both of those subjects. The instant she spotted my face peering around the corner, she broke off the general "Help! Where *is* everybody?" shouting and yelled: "Joe!"

"I'll get help," I yelled back, feeling more foolish than usual as I started to turn and gallop toward the stairs I had spotted not far from the elevators.

"No!" she shouted back, stopping me in my tracks and bringing me back to the corridor. "They want the disk!" she shouted as I reappeared. "Catch! It's in here!"

With that, she let go of the purse and it went flying over the heads of the two apes and above the wavery spot in the air. I reacted just fast enough to lurch into the middle of the corridor and snag the purse as it came sailing by. I didn't have to open it to know that the disk was indeed inside as Kay had said. The familiar pulsing light was seeping out through a half dozen undefined seams and folds. I wasn't sure that the whole purse wasn't glowing just a bit.

The apes, meanwhile, had faltered to a halt, and I got the distinct impression that they were confused. Maybe it was the way they turned toward each other for an instant as the purse sailed over their heads, or maybe the uncertain way they moved now, twitching toward Kay and the others one second, toward me and the purse the next. When they looked in my direction, I could see their faces were a good deal more human and less hairy than their arms and hands had led me to believe. The features were flattened, but they could pass for odd-looking humans if they just wore the right clothes—loose with long sleeves, and gloves. And they did have just five fingers per hand, I could see now.

Despite my inner urgings, I didn't renew my dash for the stairs now that I had the purse. For one thing, the two apes were making no obvious moves to chase me or even threaten me, and their hands were completely empty. For another, they kept looking back and forth between Kay and me, as though they couldn't really believe they had been outmaneuvered. If nothing else, my presence seemed to be confusing them, distracting them from Kay and the others. When I had first poked my head around the corner, the apes had been actively stalking them. Now they were simply standing there, not far from their wavery spot, doing nothing more menacing than shifting their feet nervously.

At the far end of the hall, though, Radsack's wild-eyed confusion seemed to have increased, if anything. He was still looking around frantically in all directions, even at the wall with its single window behind him. Then, abruptly, he froze, staring at the window. It took me a couple of seconds to realize what he was looking at, but finally it registered.

Something outside the window, five floors up, was glowing, and it wasn't just from all the neon signs that were coming on in the streets now that it was turning dark. This was closer and steadier and—

Radsack came unfrozen, grasping the window and tugging at it frantically, seemingly forgetting all about the apes. I could hear his grunts of exertion from my position fifty or seventy-five feet away. The window was stubborn, though, and after a couple of seconds, he began pounding at the sash on all sides and jabbing at anything that remotely resembled a catch, then went back to jerking at it, all in a matter of seconds. It was like watching one of those old, speeded-up silent movies, except there wasn't any breakneck piano tinkling in the background.

Suddenly, the window was open—really open. For an instant, the entire window—sash, glass, and all—was balancing on Radsack's finger tips, loose, and then it plummeted out of sight. Radsack, though, didn't even look down to see where the window was headed. Instead, he jammed his head and shoulders out through the opening and looked straight ahead at the fluorescent-like glow that hung in midair a dozen feet beyond the window. He yelled something, just a couple of syllables, at the top of his voice, but whatever the syllables were, I couldn't catch them, either because of the accent or because a fair amount of my attention had snapped back to the apes.

They had started to move at about the same instant the window gave way, and now they were diving headfirst toward their wavery spot, which meant they were also diving headfirst toward me. I jumped back reflexively, half expecting them to land at my feet, but they didn't.

They vanished. Of course.

At about the same time, the glow hanging in the air outside the permanently open window also vanished, and then, at a more leisurely pace, the wavery spot in the corridor stopped wavering and followed the apes and the external glow into whatever limbo they had vanished into.

Finally, Kay's purse, still clutched tightly in my hands, quit glowing at the seams. The disk must have decided to call it a day, too.

Tentatively, I glanced inside the now darkened purse but saw nothing beyond the usual jumble. Then, cautiously, I started down the hall toward Kay and the others, who were just as cautiously moving in my direction.

Kay was the first to speak as we met at approximately the spot where the apes had vanished into wavery air. She opened her mouth, and after a second a couple of words, "How did . . ." came out before she stopped, her forehead creased in a monumentally puzzled frown.

She didn't snap her fingers, but the effect was the same as her eyes suddenly widened and she spun around sharply. "Bob! Bob Adams! Where did *he* get to?"

"*He* was here, too?" I asked automatically. "Don't tell me he disappeared again?"

I looked toward Don, who seemed to be recovering his composure to a degree, and wondered if finally seeing Adams disappear before his very eyes, as advertised, was what had shaken him up so much rather than seeing the two apes.

Kay frowned, shaking her head. "I *think* he was here, but . . ."

"You *think* he was? What's that supposed to mean?"

"It means just what it says," she snapped, her eyes roaming around the corridor the same way Radsack's had roamed a few minutes earlier.

"But if he's here now," I said, "he's scared, which means you ought to be able to locate him if your dowsing equipment is in working order. You did it often enough last year."

She blinked, shaking her head. "Wrong phase of the moon, or maybe it doesn't work outside the continental U.S.," she said, but the words sounded mechanical, as if her mind was still somewhere else. Then her eyes fell on Don, who had been looking around apprehensively himself.

"Yes!" she said abruptly. "He *was* with us! Don, you must remember—the two of you were in his room, right there." She pointed toward the next to last door in the dead-end corridor. "You said you'd been working on your next *Midnight Inquirer* article or something like that. You *do* remember, don't you?"

Now Don was frowning, looking around puzzledly. "I *think* I do, but . . . Yes, you're right!" His voice went up a notch in pitch. "We—we were just finishing up some notes when you knocked on the door. I remember now, but . . ."

"Adams?" Now it was Radsack who was frowning puzzledly. "What are you two talking about? You were alone when I—" Radsack blinked. "You *were* alone, weren't you? Just you and Don?"

His voice sounded uncertain, and once again I thought I noticed a decrease in the thickness of his accent. He was adapting to Yank visitors? Come to think of it, the only time he had really lapsed into an almost impenetrable accent or used a lot of entries from my slang dictionary was last night, when he had been involved with Gary . . .

Don, seeming to notice Radsack's proximity for the first time, moved away, his eyes darting nervously over the gangling Australian.

"I—I don't know," Don said hesitantly, the admission obviously being made with a huge effort. "I thought I was, but . . ." Doubt, or maybe incipient panic, worked its way into his face. "I just don't know!"

Then something flickered in my peripheral vision, and I darted a look toward the end of the corridor. As I looked, Adams faded into existence. He was standing near the window, wearing his usual rumpled brown suit like an untidy uniform.

Kay breathed a sigh of relief as she saw him, and then shot an annoyed glance at Don. "Let's see your magical phonies do *that!*"

"What? Do what?" Don looked around, and then he, too, saw Adams. He was silent a moment, his roundish face working its way from shock to confusion.

At the same time, Radsack had looked around, and his reaction was similar to Don's but much more pronounced. Even behind the beard, it was obvious that his mouth sagged open. He took a step backward, stopping when he bumped into me.

"I remember now . . ." Radsack's voice was a whisper, and his eyes, always large, were beginning to look like Marty Feldman's. "I remember . . ."

Radsack's hands shot out, grasping at Don's arms. "He *was* with you!" Despite the emphasis, Radsack's words managed to convey the feeling that he desperately wanted Don to contradict him.

But Don didn't. He only looked blank for a moment, and then, with a shudder, jerked away from Radsack's clutching hands.

Radsack didn't seem to notice Don's reaction to his touch. He only looked around at Kay and me, and I thought for a second he was going to grab one or both of us next. In the meantime, Adams had approached our little cluster unsteadily, apologetically. Now, as the rumpled little man came to a hesitant stop a couple of feet away, Radsack began to back away.

Kay, relaxing a bit now that Adams was again visible and none the worse for wear, finally noticed Radsack's apparent terror at the little man's approach.

"Don't drop your bundle, mate," she said in a fair imitation of Radsack's own words to Gary the night before. "He does that every so often."

Radsack's eyes darted toward her, but they kept returning to Adams, who was still keeping a respectful couple of yards between himself and the rest of us.

"But he—he just vanished!" Radsack's voice was a horrified whisper.

Kay laughed suddenly, and an instant later, as I realized why, I joined her.

"For someone who vanished *himself* less than twenty-four hours ago," she said, "you're taking this pretty hard, aren't you? And you saw that six-fingered bloke, twice Bob's size—"

"But that was different! That was—" Abruptly, Radsack stopped. His whole body and face were motionless, and it reminded me of those freeze-frame shots they've been using at the ends of movies and TV dramas so much lately. The motion all of a sudden stops, except for the credits as they roll across the screen. No credits were superimposed on Radsack's face, but the way things had been going, it wouldn't have surprised me all that much if they had been. Although I can't imagine who would want to take credit for the last twenty-four hours, come to think of it. Certainly no one in Kay's group.

Finally, after at least five seconds of being a pop-eyed, open-mouthed statue, Radsack came to life. His mouth clapped shut so fast I'm sure I heard his teeth click. Then he blinked once, swallowed, and said:

"I've got to go."

And he went. No "So long, see you later," or anything like that. He just went, at a shambling trot, and vanished into a stair-well, the door swishing shut behind him, cutting off his echoing footsteps.

"What was *that* all about?" Kay asked of the world in general as she turned away from the stairwell door and looked toward the rest of us.

Don, who seemed to have switched from nervous twitchiness to nervous aggressiveness now that Radsack was gone, shook his head, frowning in annoyance. "How should I know? Good riddance, if you ask me. That guy gets on my nerves."

"I've noticed," Kay said, "and to tell the truth, I've been meaning to ask you about that."

"Ask me about what?" There was definitely a belligerent tone to Don's voice.

"I've noticed it, too," I put in. "You practically jumped out of your skin just now when he touched you."

"Is that your cliché for the day, Karns?" he snapped. "'Out of your skin'! Beautiful. I hope your travel articles turn out better than that or they'll stick me with writing them after all!"

I was a little taken aback. Don wasn't usually that much on the attack.

"You *have* been acting pretty jumpy, Don," Kay said, unintimidated, "ever since you first met Radsack last night. What is it that—"

"He's just a troublemaker, that's all!" Don said sharply, but there was still a trace of a puzzled frown creasing his abundant forehead. He turned away from Kay and me then, as if to get away from an uncomfortable topic. He moved toward Adams, still standing by unobtrusively. He stared at the little man for a moment.

"We—we were in your room a few minutes ago, weren't we?" Don asked uncertainly. "Working on that new article?"

Bob Adams nodded. "You said you were just about finished. You—" He gestured hesitantly toward Don's checked sport jacket. "You put your notebook in your pocket."

Don blinked, then lowered his eyes to look uncertainly at the front of his jacket. Slowly he reached inside and pulled out a small, spiral-bound notebook. I could see memory crawling back across his face as he looked at the notebook, then flipped it open and slid his eyes rapidly down the scribbled pages.

"Yes," Don said finally, uncertainly. "I . . . remember now. Of course."

"I'm sorry," Adams said softly.

"Sorry? No, it's just that I—" He shook his head violently, as if trying to physically dislodge the offending memories. "I remember it, now that I see my notes, but . . ." His voice trailed away in confusion.

"I know," Adams said, still so softly as to be nearly inaudible. "It happened like this once before, when I was little."

"It was like *this* before?" Kay asked, a sudden eagerness in her voice. "You not only disappeared, but people forgot about you?"

Adams lowered his head in a not-quite nod. "Once, when I was a little boy, and this huge dog came charging out from a driveway. It wasn't like when the other kids would run at me. I mean, they would scare me all right, and I think I disappeared a few times, but this time— That dog was as big as I was, and he was running right at me. I guess I disappeared, because the dog sort of went right past me, only now he was barking at my father. I'd been running ahead, and my father was a little ways behind me. The dog must not've been really mean, though, just noisy, and my father chased him away. But then my father must've forgotten I was there. He just looked around a little and then started walking back home, fast. I chased him and yelled, but I guess he couldn't hear me, either. Anyway, I had to run all the way to keep up with him."

"What did he say when you reappeared?" Kay wondered.

Adams shook his head, still keeping his eyes downcast. "Nothing much. He still couldn't see me when we got home, and I just went up to my room and laid down for a while. I was really scared then. I was afraid they'd never be able to see me again, and that just made it worse, I guess. Finally I fell asleep, though, and when I woke up, my mother was standing in the doorway, watching me. She looked kind of funny at first, but then she ran over and hugged me, and everything was all right again."

Adams looked up at Kay. "After that, I tried my best not to do it any more. It was sort of like being a ghost." He shivered faintly.

"I can imagine," Kay said, but then she glanced toward me. "See, I told you that was how it worked."

I looked at her blankly, and so did Don.

"Don't you get it?" she asked incredulously. "Remember, I *said* he doesn't *really* disappear, he just clouds men's minds, you should excuse the expression."

"And the forgetting is just the next step?" I asked as the idea filtered into my mind. "First he clouds our minds so we can't see him, and then, if it gets really bad, he clouds them some more, and we can't even remember he was here in the first place?"

"Right! And now it's wearing off." Kay turned back to Adams. "Were you just more frightened this time? Is that how it works?"

"Maybe. Those creatures were— Well, the way they popped out of nowhere that way, and they were so close, it *was* sort of like that dog that time."

Adams looked down at his feet again, which, though they

weren't actually moving, gave the impression of scuffing in non-existent dirt. "And to tell the truth," he went on, "I was actually trying this time. I actually thought, 'I *want* to disappear!'"

Kay grinned triumphantly. "Induced hysterical blindness, followed by temporary amnesia! Beautiful!"

She looked toward Don, who had been taking it all in silently. "I'm remembering more of it all the time," she said. "I think it's just about all back, although— How about you?"

"Yes, but—" Don began, then looked uncertainly toward Adams. "Then those fairy tales of yours are for real?"

Kay laughed, a decidedly amused sound, and even Adams smiled a little. "You really thought we were imagining all those things last year?" she asked.

Don shook his head. "Frankly, yes. I just couldn't—" He frowned abruptly, nervously. "But those others, that thing last night, and those silver-suited apes just now? You mean *they're* real, too?"

"You thought we were having mass hallucinations?" Kay asked, still grinning.

"No, but . . . But *they* didn't just disappear, not like him." Don glanced nervously at Adams again. "They were different. They . . . went away somewhere."

"Like Bob's brother James did," Kay said. "Teleportation of some sort, that's all."

"That's *all?* You make it sound like it happens every day! Where's your—your sense of wonder?"

"Where's yours? You didn't even believe it was happening at all until a few seconds ago."

"That's different. I was—" Don stopped, almost as abruptly and completely as Radsack had when he had gone into his freeze-frame pose, and his eyes went blank for a moment, as if a curtain had been pulled down for a fast scene change on his mental stage. Then his eyes lighted up, literally, although I assume it must have been an odd reflection of the overhead lights in the corridor as he moved his head.

"If I can just get proof . . ." I could imagine the wheels turning in Don's head as he spoke. He turned back to Adams and put on his best smile.

"You say this time you actually *tried* to disappear?" he asked.

"This was the first time since you've been an adult that it happened this way?"

Don put a friendly arm across Adams' shoulders, apparently forgetting about Kay and me altogether, not to mention the silver-suited apes that had rattled his cage so violently only minutes before.

As Adams nodded agreement, Don's smile broadened, and his arm across Adams' shoulders became a guide as Don started at a leisurely but inexorable pace back toward Adams' room.

"Why don't we get a few more notes down on this," Don was saying as they moved away down the corridor, "while it's still fresh in our minds? All right? Maybe we can figure this thing out a little better . . ."

Kay and I watched for a moment. "I think Don's sense of wonder has been superseded by his sense of money to be made," she said as the two disappeared into Adams' room.

"I can believe it," I said. "And to tell the truth, I almost envy him, being able to shut out all the rest of this stuff."

I felt Kay's hand on my arm. "Are you sure about that?" she asked.

A shiver ran up my spine in the best cliché fashion, and I'm not sure if it was from the surge of memories of disappearing giants and the rest or if it was from the hand on my arm. Either way, I hunched my shoulders forward to get rid of the tingle and shook my head slightly.

"No, I guess not," I admitted. "Incidentally, did Radsack ever get in touch with his panicky electronics expert again?"

"Gary? No, as far as I know, he didn't. And I can't. I don't think we ever got his last name, and I certainly don't remember the address."

"I didn't notice the address either, but I could find the house again if I had to."

"You recorded the trip, as usual?"

I nodded. "Along with everything else. But is it worth a trip over there to see if he's at home and if we can get something out of him if he is?"

"Oh?" She eyed me speculatively. "You're starting to sound investigative again. I thought all this was just a temporary impediment in the way of your travel articles."

Which it was, really, but, assuming everything that had happened had been real, that was sort of like saying that World War II was an impediment to your annual Paris vacation. Of course there was not much your average Paris vacationer could have done about the war, and there was probably just about as much that I could do about the giants and the apes and all the rest. But that was logic, and logic, I suspected, was totally out of place around here. Or perhaps it was just that logic and my so-called serendipity were mutually exclusive. All of which is just a meandering way of getting around to admitting that, logic or no logic, I was hooked, which is roughly what I told Kay.

"Glad to hear it," she said, "and if Radsack doesn't put in another appearance before morning, maybe a trip to Gary's place would be in order. I'd just as soon not make the trek at night again, though."

"Agreed. But why didn't Radsack call him back today? I thought he said he was going to."

Kay shrugged. "Maybe he did, but I wasn't able to find him all day—until I ran into him in the hallway here, about thirty seconds before the apes arrived, and we didn't have much time for chatting after that."

She looked around. "I wonder where he went in such a hurry? He disappears almost as fast as Adams."

"Home, maybe?" I asked. "He does live in Sydney, doesn't he?"

"He's supposed to, but the only address anybody ever had for him was a post office box. I can't even find him in the phone book."

"What about your disk? Have you shown it to anyone else?"

"A few people here, and I took it to a couple of TV-radio repair shops."

"And . . . ?"

"They looked at me like I was a ratbag."

"Ratbag?" That was one I hadn't come across in my Australian-English primer.

She laughed. "My favorite Australian word so far. Politely translated, eccentric. Klutzy weirdo. What you thought we all were at the convention last year. And probably still do, for all I know."

"But did they tell you anything useful about the disk?" I asked, tactfully avoiding comment on Kay's opinion.

"Not a thing. It wouldn't do anything for them, just laid there like a lump. Someone suggested getting it X-rayed, which I may try yet."

The elevator arrived, and a few minutes later, without either of us really having invited the other to dinner, we found ourselves in the hotel coffee shop again. While I did my best to adjust to the fact that my hamburger was served with a fried egg on top of it, Kay nibbled at her salad and continued the speculations that had gotten started in the elevator and had been going on continuously since. Most of the speculations were Kay's, of course, and they ranged from the simply implausible through the impossible to the downright ridiculous. The only thing most of them had in common was the fact that they were dredged up from the hundreds or thousands of "aliens are amongst us" stories she had read and seen over the years.

The only worthwhile conclusion we came to was that there must be two groups—the six-fingered giants and the silver-suited apes, for lack of better identification. The apes wanted Kay's disk, which had been given to her by the giants. Beyond that, there was the probability that the apes, at least, weren't too well organized or maybe just weren't too bright, considering the way they had shuffled their feet in confusion after Kay had thrown her purse over their heads to me. That particular speculation led to thoughts of degenerate, Shaverian descendants of once powerful races making poor use of the equipment built by their ancestors, which led to poorly programmed robots, which led to blockheaded warriors stumbling onto some still-operable equipment from another civilization, which led to dimensional doors, which led to the wavery spots in the air, which led to parallel worlds, which led to time travel, which led to—

But you get the idea. Everything led to something else, and it was a long and speculative evening which, in the end, led nowhere.

Nowhere that made any sense, anyway.

"What do you mean, Artil, he disappeared?"
"I mean precisely what I said: He disappeared!"
"How? Did the techs slip up and snatch him instead of—"
"No! It has nothing to do with us or our techs or anything else like that! He just plain vanished! Right before my eyes! And not

only that, while he was invisible, I couldn't even remember that he had been there! I—"

"What? Artil, have you been getting into the recreational liquids again? I've warned you before, when you're on duty—"

"I've never been more clearheaded in my life! Can't you understand what I'm saying? He disappeared! I SAW HIM DISAPPEAR!"

"That's impossible."

"I'm perfectly well aware of that! That is why I am telling you about it! It's impossible, but it happened!"

"You're—you're not trying to tell me this one is real! Are you?"

"That's exactly what I'm telling you! He must be real! What other explanation can there be?"

"But it can't be! Artil, there's got to be a mistake somewhere!"

"Yes, and I think we're the ones who are making it. We've been making the same mistake for a long, long time, and now it's catching up to us."

"No, I can't accept— It must have been our Phenomena Group, that's all. They're always fooling around like that, making things appear and disappear."

"I've already asked them. They had nothing to do with it."

"Someone else is playing around, then. You know they do that, no matter how many memos we send around."

"I know, but not this time. It was not one of our gates opening up! Don't you think I would have recognized it if it had been?"

"Perhaps, but you said you were having trouble remembering what happened anyway."

"That's not what I said! Now I can remember! It was just at the time—"

"Hypnosis? I've heard there are humans that can control minds to some extent that way."

"You just refuse to believe it, don't you, sir? You're going to go ahead with this scheme, no matter—"

"Of course we're going ahead! Don't you think that— Is that it? Artil, have you finally realized that these humans you selected are actually not suited to your plan? Is this your way of getting out from under your responsibility? If it is—"

"No! I told you the truth! If only you hadn't wandered away from the screen, you would have seen it for yourself!"

"I can hardly sit there monitoring your activities every minute, now can I? I do find it suspicious, though, that this so-called disappearance occurred during one of my few absences, now that I think about it."

"I'm sorry if you feel that way, sir, but that doesn't change anything! He still disappeared!"

"You can tell me the truth, Artil. Tell me now, before we get into this any deeper, and I won't hold it against you. It won't go in the record."

"Sir, I didn't—"

"Last chance. Admit it now, and we'll forget the whole episode."

"Sir!"

"Very well, Artil. It's on your head. I see no need for further discussion if you have nothing further to report."

"He disappeared! He really disappeared! He—"

"You have nothing more? Very well."

"But, sir— All right, if you refuse to understand, there's nothing more I can do. I can only—"

"Everything else is working correctly? You have no complaints about the work the techs are doing?"

"No, sir, I— Yes, as a matter of fact, I do! And you had better talk to them about it before someone gets killed. If I hadn't gotten to that window and yelled at them in time— They were supposed to open that gate inside the corridor, not outside in midair! If one of them had stepped through without looking, that would have been that. And the two on the inside weren't very well prepared, either, if you ask me. Most of the time, they just stood there! They were supposed to be menacing! If the rest of the crew don't do any better than that tomorrow night, maybe we had better forget the whole thing! There are worse things than being sacked, after all. And now, if you'll excuse me, sir, I had better get back there before something really goes wrong. Good day, sir!"

VIII

"I'm in No Shape to Save the World Tonight"

It doesn't take quite as long to adjust to the impossible (like glowing disks and silver-suited apes and wavery air) as it does to adjust to a new time zone, especially one that is eight hours away from what you're used to. Which is why, though my watch said it was barely ten o'clock in the evening, my head, when it was speaking to me, said it was more like dawn and was irritably badgering me to get back to my room and get some sleep. It didn't say anything at all when the phone rang a couple of hours later, and it turned out to be Kay excitedly telling me that her disk was talking to her.

When I asked what it was saying, she said she couldn't put it on the phone but that if I wanted to hear it myself I should get the lead out and get down to her room, fast.

That is not the best way to be wakened out of a sound sleep, but it is certainly one of the most effective. Unshaven and with shirttail flapping, I was down the stairwell and in the corridor leading to Kay's room in maybe three minutes. The door to her room was open, and I could hear a buzz of conversation as soon as I emerged from the stairwell. What was the disk doing, holding a press conference?

Which wasn't as wild a guess as I had thought when I made it. Kay's room was filled with people. I spotted most of the faces from the plane, plus a lot of new ones and a few I'd seen casually around the hotel. Australian fans, I assumed. The two nearest the door were obviously Australian and proud of it. Their accents made Radsack's and Eric's sound like something from a New England diction school, and I didn't even try to make out anything they were saying. As I worked my way into the room, though, I began to encounter snatches of U.S. English.

". . . obviously a teeny-tiny CB radio."

"That size? Where's the antenna?"

"Solid state, of course. You know these radios everyone's making now, that look like books or telephones or rolls of toilet paper . . ."

". . . and inside is this very tiny LP record . . ."

". . . obviously mass hallucination."

"Get another one like that, and we could open a discotalk."

". . . reminds me of the Speaking Cross which dominated the religion of Yucatán in the 1860s . . ." Denver must've been in the room somewhere, though I couldn't see him.

". . . pot in the air ducts, and I'm really lying in my room dreaming."

". . . just a good ventriloquist, that's all it would take."

". . . an interdimensional frisbee with a night light."

"Sure, and their big brothers are UFO's."

"Beautiful! 'In Search of Ancient Frisbee Nuts'!"

Finally, making frequent use of "Pardon me" and my elbows, I worked my way far enough into the room to find Kay sitting on the bed with the disk in one hand. Sure enough, the disk was glowing softly and steadily and a voice was coming out of it. And it wasn't the tinny sort of voice you'd expect from something that small, but something that made it sound as if the speaker were right there in the room. The voice was deep and resonant and had an accent that didn't sound Australian or like any other country I could think of. The word order was something else again.

". . . therefore," the disk was saying as I wedged myself onto the bed next to Kay, "Earthpeoples must aroused be to the dangers of—"

"Wait a minute," Kay said to the disk as she looked around and saw me. The disk, which apparently could hear as well as talk and glow, obligingly fell silent.

"This thing," Kay said, "says we're being invaded by aliens from another galaxy."

"From that far away?" someone on Kay's other side asked. "Why pick on us?"

"Dimensionally convenient it is," the disk resumed, confirming the fact that it could indeed hear us. "In three dimensions, distant we are from you. But in four, far closer we are. The same it is for Porovians."

"The apes," Kay interjected for my benefit. "The giants are from Ormazd; they're the good guys, according to the disk here."

"Ormazd?" a voice somewhere behind me asked. "You sure they aren't from Volta? That grammar sure sounds familiar."

After an uncertain hesitation, the disk continued. "Control fields Porovians have established, for us great difficulty causing."

And so it went. Despite the continuous interruptions and sometimes impossible word order, the rest of the disjointed story came out. The Porovian apes were "marauders" and they had gotten here first and had established some sort of energy field that prevented the Ormazdan giants from coming and going freely. So far, the Ormazdans had only managed a couple of breakthroughs and might not be able to manage any more. The one Ormazdan that had managed to come through physically had left the disk with Kay before the Porovians had forced him back. The disk was a combination communicator and detector. It was supposed to start pulsing whenever one of the Porovian "doors" opened up nearby.

Once all this had laboriously come out, I got around to asking something that seemed like an obvious question. "How do you know our language?"

"Monitoring your radio broadcasts have we been," came the reply, and I noticed that there was a curious stereo effect that hadn't been there previously. It took me a second to realize that someone behind me had been chorusing the answer right along with the disk. When I looked around, Denny was standing there grinning toothily.

"The next line is 'To your leader me take,'" he said.

"Your leaders must they—" the disk began, then stopped as if it had just heard Denny and was confused.

"I doubt if our leaders would believe you," Kay told the disk.

"Realize that we do," the disk said promptly, as if this was something it was prepared for. "Porovian captured must be, and to your leaders taken. Believe then they will."

"But even if they believed it, what could they do?" Kay asked, but the disk didn't seem to have heard. The glow began to fade.

"Control field interfering is," the disk said, its voice fading with the glow until, with a couple of final, unintelligible mumbles, both were gone.

"Is it over?" someone asked.

"Looks like it," another voice responded. "Wonder where we get the audience response cards to fill out?"

From those and innumerable other comments in a similar vein, it was obvious that no one believed a word the disk had said, and now that the show was over, the room began to drain into the hall like a giant sinus.

Despite all the jokes and disbelief, though, I couldn't help but get a cold, uncomfortable feeling in my stomach as, along with Kay, I silently watched the disk, wondering if it was indeed through for the night. My mind told me it was impossible, just as everyone in the room had insisted, but still . . .

If people could disappear before your eyes, if disks could talk, if apes in silver suits and giants with six fingers could leap in and out of splotches of wavery air, then what was so impossible about an invasion from another galaxy? Sure, it was a cliché, but who said a cliché had to be impossible? Everyone who had been in the room besides Kay and myself, that's who.

It was, I realized, the same sort of feeling you get when you're face to face with something that "just can't happen" to you. Like that *Clarion* writer who had rolled his car over on the expressway had said. You see that car stalled in front of you, and you realize a half second later that there's no way in the world you can stop in time, and a half second after that you're going sideways down the road and then starting to roll over in the median strip. It's impossible, but it's happening, and what can you do about it? Not a thing, except promise yourself to be more careful next time, if there is a next time, and be eternally grateful that you fastened your safety belt and are driving a car with good, solid side pillars holding up the roof.

But here there wasn't any safety belt or side pillars, unless you counted that glowing and talking disk with the inverted grammar. Or maybe the real safety belt was simple disbelief. Everyone else in the room had certainly used it and seemed to have survived nicely.

Finally, the room was empty, and as the last hangers-on meandered into the hallway, Radsack charged through the door.

"Somebody said the disk started talking!" he said excitedly as he lurched to a halt.

"Started and stopped," Kay told him, holding up the now defunct disk.

He looked down at it, his eyes wide. "It's a radio, then? Who was it? What did they say?"

"Whoever it was said we were being invaded," Kay said, and went on to give him a brief summary while I watched and wondered. Wondered things like, where had Radsack been while the disk had been talking? And where had he disappeared to the instant after he found out about Adams' ability to vanish? And why didn't he have an address besides a post office box?

Then Kay was done summarizing and Radsack was looking crestfallen. "You mean you're the only ones who took it seriously?" he asked, his eyes wide with disbelief as he looked from the disk to Kay and then to me.

"Looks that way," Kay said, and I noticed that she was beginning to sound a little tired. "And if you must know, I'm not so sure about myself."

"But you saw—"

"Let's not go through that again," she said, a little sharply, and I wondered if she was having the same sort of reaction to Radsack that Don had been having.

"Well, whatever we believe," I put in, "maybe we should put that thing away somewhere for the night. Like in the hotel safe."

"But why?" It was Radsack objecting, not Kay.

"For one thing," I explained, "if any of this is true, then those extradimensional apes are after it, and they're enough to disturb anyone's sleep, and maybe their health."

"But it will warn you! It said—"

"A lot of good that will do me," Kay said. "It blinked its head off this evening, and it didn't do much good." Definitely snappish. I figured things were getting to her. Monsters. Invasions from other galaxies. Talking disks. Bad jokes. "Maybe *you* should keep it for a while if you're so anxious," she finished, holding the disk out to Radsack.

He started to object, but then cut himself short. "Sure," he said, "if that's what you really want."

"It is." She tossed the disk to him, and he caught it clumsily.

"If it comes out with any emergency instructions for me before morning, you take care of them, okay? I'm not in any shape to save the world tonight."

The next thing I knew, the door was closing behind us. "See you in the morning, Joe," Kay was saying, which I guess meant that I wasn't in quite the same class as Radsack despite the fact that we were both being hustled into the hall.

Radsack looked uncertainly at the disk still in his hand, then at me, then at a cluster of fans still chatting a dozen yards down the hall. Finally, with a look of resignation, he dropped the disk in his trouser pocket and we started toward the elevator, away from the fans, who were clustered around a stairwell entrance.

We were almost at the elevator when Radsack, an almost pleading note in his voice, asked: "*Why* don't they believe it? Do *you* have any idea?"

The tone, if not the question, startled me a bit. "I thought they pretty well covered that last night," I said.

"Rusty, you mean? I know what he said, but—" Radsack shook his head and dispiritedly jabbed at the elevator button. "But they've seen and heard so much! I just don't see how they can *not* believe it. But you—*you* believe it, don't you?"

I shrugged. Radsack looked stricken at my apparent lack of commitment.

"I believe *something* is happening," I admitted. "It's like the UFO's. Something is going on, but I'm not sure what, no more than anyone else is. But tell me, why are you so dead set on it yourself? Don't you have any doubts at all?"

"Of course not," he said. "After all, I am—" He stopped abruptly, his lips frozen in the process of forming the next word. Another freeze-frame, I thought. He blinked, then shook his head.

"Yes?" I prompted. "You are what?"

Radsack's mouth opened again, as if to speak, but there was only silence. Then his mouth snapped shut. A frown creased his forehead behind the black hair that was falling loosely over it.

"Is something wrong?" I asked.

He shook his head sharply. "No! I just—" Again he stopped. The frown deepened and his eyes widened.

Just then the elevator door slid open.

"Good evening." It wasn't the elevator talking, though it wouldn't have surprised me much if it had been. Instead, it was a tiny, gray-haired woman, at least in her sixties, maybe older. She was wearing a scarlet pantsuit and was smiling broadly at both Radsack and myself. I nodded to her and, a moment later, so did Radsack, although his was more of a nervous twitch than a nod. We started to get into the elevator.

Radsack hesitated halfway in, and the doors clumped their rubber bumpers against his shoulders and cycled open again.

"Are you all right, young man?" The gray-haired woman, her movements quick and unhesitating, stepped to the front of the car and put a steadying hand on Radsack's arm.

His eyes darted down toward her, and I could see his lips twitch, as if he were fighting to keep the words inside. "No," he began, "I—I just—"

Abruptly, he clamped his mouth shut so hard his teeth clacked together. Then he stepped, almost leaped, backward out of the elevator.

"I'll see you in the morning." The words shot out of his mouth through lips that barely moved. "I—I feel a little—a little strange."

He was turning away, in the direction of the stairwell, when the door slid shut again. I thought for a second of going after him, but then I found myself wondering if whatever was afflicting him could be the result of the disk starting to act up again. After all, he did have it in his pocket. For once, my upstairs observer, a rational soul who told me firmly to mind my own business, won out, if only by default. By the time my less rational self had decided that maybe I should really go chasing after Radsack, if only to see if he needed help, the elevator was on its way up, and it was easy enough to convince myself that even if I got off on the next floor and ran back down the stairs, I wouldn't be able to find him. Besides, he hadn't looked so much sick as he had scared.

"Do you think your friend will be all right? He looked a bit peaked to me."

I looked around, startled. Somehow, in only three or four seconds, I had been completely distracted from the woman in the elevator with me.

"I think he's all right," I said, and then surprised myself by adding: "He's just a little strange, that's all. Besides, I doubt that I could catch up with him now, anyway."

She nodded, a small, birdlike motion. "You're probably right. He did seem terribly nervous about something."

"He was," I agreed. "He definitely was. I only wish I knew—" I broke off. Whoever this woman was, she wasn't going to be interested in my problems with Radsack and the rest. And even if she were, they were hardly any of her business, and I definitely wasn't the type to confide in casual strangers.

She was nodding again, I noticed, more slowly now, and her smile seemed even friendlier than before. Her eyes were remarkably clear and blue, and then I wondered why I had noticed something as irrelevant as that. I *never* noticed the color of people's eyes. If it wasn't for the blank I have to fill in on my driver's license application every so often, I wouldn't even know the color of my own.

Then we were at my floor, the eighth, and the door was opening. I started to get out, then hesitated, possessed of a sudden, inexplicable urge to say "so long" or "see you later" or just to wave to her. She was still smiling, and I couldn't help wondering if Mary Worth had a skinny sister.

"My name is Maydene Cartlin, by the way," she said.

"Joe Karns," I said as the door bumpers clumped against me and recycled.

"Very nice to meet you," she said. She didn't offer her hand, but I felt, inside, as if we had already shaken hands. Warmly, even affectionately. It was a strange feeling. "I hope we'll have a chance to talk longer sometime, Mr. Karns."

I blinked, then shook my head and made an extra effort to move. I barely avoided the door bumpers as the door slid shut and blocked out Maydene Cartlin's still-smiling face.

My upstairs observer and I both wondered what new impossibility we had stumbled into, and neither of us had the faintest idea, although I had a sneaky suspicion that we'd be finding out before long. With six-fingered giants and talking disks and silver-suited apes on the scene, it was only to be expected that a little old lady with a strange aura about her would show up . . .

"Artil? Are you there? Can you talk now?"

"Yes, Maurtiss, I can talk. What is it?"

"I was listening. It didn't go very well—did it?

"Not very well, no sir. But the four of them—"

"Four? I could find only two."

"The other two weren't there, but I'm sure they're convinced. But I still feel this whole affair should be canceled. The one—"

"I know, Artil. He disappears. Is that all?"

"Yes, sir, that is— No, it isn't all. Something else happened. Someone—"

"Someone else disappeared? Who was it this time?"

"No, sir, no one else disappeared. It was just this elderly female, sir. She . . ."

"Yes? She what?"

"It's hard to explain, sir. It's just that I found myself almost blurting out the truth to her."

"It would hardly seem to matter one way or the other, Artil. No one has believed anything you've said so far anyway."

"I beg your pardon—"

"I don't know what you're trying to pull, Artil, but let me warn you—it won't work. If you want to back out now, just say so. It's late, but it can still be done."

"No, sir, it's not that. I just—"

"Very well. Then carry on. Have your group at the spot on time. Do you think you can manage at least that much?"

"Yes, sir, but—"

"Good. I will look forward to speaking to you again—after Bondeach has left."

IX

"I'd Never Have Made It on Social Security"

I got up fairly early the next morning for a couple of reasons. In the first place, I still wasn't adjusted to the time, and something inside me thought it was already the middle of the afternoon. In the second place, I figured I had better check in with Mike, and if I waited much longer, he would either have gone home for the night or tried to call me.

When I finally got him, I hastily skimmed over my more or less legitimate activities of the past days, leaving out anything more exotic than the bandicoots and the like in the zoo. I didn't bother mentioning the zoo I had run into on the plane or any of the other oddities. All Mike was interested in was whether or not I was sticking to the schedule, article-wise. Once I assured him I was, he lost interest, probably because he—or the *Clarion*, with which he identified strongly—was paying for the call.

I was in the hotel coffee shop, trying to match my expense account to the menu, when, not too surprisingly, Maydene Cartlin appeared across the table from me. She was still smiling, though not quite as widely as the night before, and I wondered if it was the same one or if she started a fresh one each day. At least she wasn't wearing the same scarlet pantsuit. Today's was sky blue.

Before I was fully aware of inviting her to join me, she was sitting down and I was grinning back at her. Whatever aura had been hovering around her last night was still hovering, only maybe not quite as strong. Or maybe she was diverting part of it to a nearby waitress, because one showed up within seconds of the time she sat down.

After being assured by the waitress that what she was looking at was indeed the breakfast menu, she ordered steak and eggs, and from the motherly way she looked at me, I suspected even then that before the meal was over, she would be slicing off a hunk of steak and sliding it across to my plate along with an admonition that it would "just go to waste" otherwise. I was my usual adventurous self and ordered ham and eggs.

"You're from America, Mr. Karns?" she asked when the waitress had departed.

I nodded and named the midwest city I'd lived in the last few years.

"And what do you do?" The words sounded like Lesson No. 1 in a Dale Carnegie course: Develop and display a sincere interest in the other person. But either she had learned the lesson exceedingly well, or . . .

"I'm with the *Clarion*," I told her, and then found myself saying, "I'm subbing for the travel editor, doing some articles for him on Australia."

"How interesting." The cliché reply, but from her I believed it. I wished I could sound that sincere. My interviews for articles might go better than they usually did if I sounded like that.

Somehow, with very little prompting from her, I found myself spilling out the whole sordid story, from Werner's aversion to travel to my Harbour Bridge traffic jam. I even considered telling her about the silver-suited apes and the disk, but sanity prevailed, at least temporarily. All through my ramblings, she kept right on smiling, looking incredibly interested in every word, and making remarks that indicated she was actually hearing what I was saying. I kept telling myself, between paragraphs, that it must be an act, but if it was, it was the best one I'd ever seen.

When I finally ran down, the food was arriving, and I was just as glad. If I hadn't had something to do with my mouth besides talk, I probably *would* have started chattering about invading aliens.

When she had, as I had expected her to, passed me a chunk of her steak and was watching me finish it off, she said: "I'm a writer, too, in a way."

"Oh?" Romance novels, I thought, but then remembered seeing an article about one sweet little old lady whose private eye books could turn Mickey Spillane green with envy, although her name hadn't been Cartlin. "What sort of writing?" I asked politely.

She shook her head in self-deprecation. "I probably shouldn't tell you, but I write for the 'confessions.'"

"Confessions?" I almost added that she didn't look Catholic, but I restrained myself.

"You know. You've seen the magazines, I'm sure. *True Confessions, Real Romances, Intimate Secrets,* and a couple dozen others."

I continued munching on the steak, unsure of what to say. It was kind of like discovering that Mary Worth was really a sex therapist, or maybe a porno writer on the side. I shouldn't have been surprised, though. Even Don Thompson had, in a weak moment, confided that he had written them occasionally to pick up some extra money and to get out of the "who-what-when-where-why" strait jacket of the news story format. He had even managed to find a couple of markets that used fantasies, which I gather was rare in that field. Considering the titles he mentioned, I could see a reason for the rarity. My personal favorite had always been "A Ghost Made My Husband Impotent!" He never said whether he'd been able to sell that one or not.

"There's no need to be embarrassed," she assured me, apparently misinterpreting my uncommunicative attack on the last bits of steak. "They're really rather fun to do. And even if they won't make me rich, I've done enough of them in the last few years to save up for this trip. I'd never have made it on social security, you can be sure."

"It's not that," I hastened to assure her as the last steak morsel went down. "It's just a little unexpected. It takes me a minute to shift gears, so to speak."

Something new was added to her smile. I hesitate to call it a twinkle in her eye, but I can't think what else to call it.

"I know," she said, nodding daintily. "And it's just as much fun telling people about them as it is to write them. My goodness, you would be surprised how many people think those stories are true. I imagine it must be all those 'trues' and 'reals' in the magazine titles that fool them."

"Yes, that could tend to mislead you, if you're a bit gullible.

But don't they sometimes—" There I went again. I had been about to ask her if there wasn't at least a germ of truth in any of the stories, and then launch into how Don had once used something the *Clarion*'s overly macho "outdoor writer" had told him, supposedly in confidence, in one of his confessions and had almost got punched out for it.

"Yes? You were saying?" She was looking at me again, with those impossible blue eyes.

So I told her.

She was smiling sympathetically when I finished. "I can understand why he did it, but to use what a friend told him . . . No, I could never do that. It would be too awkward."

"Then yours are totally fictional?"

"Oh no, on the contrary, they're more nearly true than most, I'm sure. Oh, I have to change things around a bit so they come out happier or more dramatically. Or to work in the proper message. Some of the magazines are very message-conscious, you know. But use what a friend told me? No, that would be quite unconscionable, unless, of course, they told me I could do it. That does happen occasionally."

"But if your stories are true . . . Don't tell me all those things happened to *you*, only with less dramatic endings?"

She laughed, and her laugh was as—well, as warm as her smile. Incredible, I thought, and some scenes from *Harold and Maude*, a movie I'd had to review a few years before, flitted uneasily through my mind.

"Goodness, no. I've lived a very quiet sort of life, I'm afraid. But people do tell me things now and again."

"You mean perfect strangers walk up to you and spill their darkest secrets?" Even as I asked the question, I suspected that I knew the answer already.

"People do tend to confide in me," she said quietly.

She really is Mary Worth, I thought, but I didn't laugh as I remembered how I had just finished telling her about Don and about how I came to be in Australia and all the rest. No deep, dark secrets, maybe, but still it wasn't the sort of thing I normally did. And even now there was a niggling urge inside of me, poking at me every so often, trying to get the words flowing again on other topics, like maybe disappearing giants or talking disks.

The scraping of chair legs on the floor brought me back to the present, and as my eyes focused and I looked toward the sound, I saw that the chair was at our table and that Kay Clarke was lowering herself into it. She looked as if a night's sleep had done her some good, and if the look on her face was any indication, she had gotten back her normal exuberance. She was even wearing something different today, totally unlike her usual slacks and sweater, and I wondered if it might not be one of her stage outfits. The brightly colored turban was bigger than the Afro concealed beneath it, and the gold earrings looked large and sturdy enough to swing from. The African-looking wrap-around that covered everything from shoulders to ankles looked like leopard-spotted fake fur at first glance but proved to be a fabric of some sort. All in all, she created quite a barbaric effect, and I imagined it would be very effective on a stage.

I introduced them, and then found myself rambling on about Kay's singing and Mrs. Cartlin's confessions and how most of them really *were* confessions from casual acquaintances like us.

"You mean they just come right out and tell you these things?" Kay asked. "You don't have to grill them, even a little bit?"

"Goodness, no! I'd never pry into someone's affairs," Mrs. Cartlin told her. "But, of course, if they want to talk, I'm willing to listen."

"But why should they tell you so much? I know that when people get drunk, they— You don't get them drunk, do you?"

Mrs. Cartlin laughed, an aged, tinkling sound. "Gracious, no! Not that I disapprove of drinking, you understand, though I've never indulged in it myself . . ." She gave the impression of shrugging, but I'm not sure that her shoulders actually moved.

"Has it always been that way?" Kay asked.

Again there was a fleeting impression of a shrug. "To some extent, I imagine. I remember when I was in school, the other girls were always telling me about their troubles with boy friends. And the boys would tell me about their troubles with girl friends . . ."

For a moment, Maydene Cartlin's eyes seemed to retreat into

the past, but they returned quickly, twinkling, darting from Kay to myself and back. "Perhaps it's my sweet, motherly face."

"Does everyone do it?" Kay persisted. I recognized her tone. It was the same one she had used last year when she was questioning me about my own "serendipity." She was onto something. Or maybe up to something.

"No, not everyone," Mrs. Cartlin said, shaking her head very slightly. "But, then, I don't suppose everyone has a secret he wants to get off his chest. And of course there are some people who simply won't say anything to me—like your friend last night," she added, her eyes darting toward me.

"Friend?" Kay asked, giving me a fast and puzzled frown.

"Radsack," I said. "We bumped into Mrs. Cartlin on the elevator after we left your room."

"He was really quite upset," Mrs. Cartlin said. "I do wonder what was bothering the poor boy."

"How could you tell something was bothering him?" Kay asked.

Mrs. Cartlin looked doubtful, but only for an instant, and then the smile was back. "I can usually tell," she said, "but I don't really know how. A way they have of looking at me, perhaps. It's a pity, really. I'm sure they would feel better if they told someone whatever it was that was bothering them. At least that's what everyone tells me, that they feel much better afterward."

"I don't doubt it," I said, noting my own discomfort at trying to hold anything back from her, "but I don't think that's the case with Radsack."

"True," Kay put in. "Radsack's already been telling everyone in sight what's bothering him. His problem is, no one believes him."

"Oh?" Mrs. Cartlin turned the full, blue twinkle of her eyes on Kay. It was no real surprise, then, when Kay, after only a brief hesitation, said:

"He's convinced that Earth is being invaded by aliens from another galaxy."

"My goodness, how odd. Usually what people tell me is precisely what they won't tell anyone else. How very odd. And he actually believes it? That we're being invaded?"

I sighed. It shouldn't have been mentioned, but it had been. And if Kay hadn't, I'm sure I would have in another minute or two. And that niggling little urge inside me was still not satisfied. It was— Well, the only thing I can think of that is anything like it is when you're watching a suspense movie, a good one, like one of Hitchcock's, and you know the killer is lurking behind the drapes. You keep wanting to shout at the hero to keep away from the drapes. You know it's dumb and useless, but the urge is there and you keep on squirming, inwardly at least, until the guy either leaves the room altogether or actually slides the drapes back and gets attacked. It can be very uncomfortable, and so was this thing inside me now.

And Kay, from the way she looked, was feeling it, too. She was trying to cover it up, but she was feeling it. Even her voice had an odd tension in it.

I thought for a moment of Radsack. The same thing must've hit him last night, only harder. That must be why he had done his sudden about face and refused to get into the elevator with Mrs. Cartlin—and her aura.

So we told her, Kay and I, in alternating pieces of slightly organized confusion, all about the disappearing giant and the silver-suited apes and the chatty, glowing disk—everything. And as we told her, the feeling went away. At least mine did. My insides settled down, and from the gradual relaxation that crept back into Kay's voice, I assume that hers did, too.

Mrs. Cartlin sat silently, except for an occasional "My goodness," through the entire recital, soaking it up like a gray-haired, blue-eyed sponge. When we finished, she gave us a final "My gracious!" and looked thoughtful.

"You know," she said after several seconds of post-recital silence, "it all sounds like something I read once. You wouldn't remember it, you're much too young, but it was back in the thirties, I think."

"Read it? In a newspaper, you mean?" I couldn't imagine what a story like that would be doing in a newspaper back then, a decade before Kenneth Arnold started the flying saucer craze, but when you work for a newspaper the way I do, you sometimes tend to forget that other forms of the printed word exist.

"A newspaper?" Mrs. Cartlin looked at me blankly for a second. "What— Oh, I see what you mean!" She laughed, and I noticed that Kay was grinning, too.

"Goodness, no," she went on. "That sort of thing never made the newspapers then. No, it was in a scientifiction magazine, of course."

It took me a moment to dredge up a definition of scientifiction —a clumsy-sounding word if ever I heard one—that one of Kay's condescending friends had dropped on me at the convention last year. An archaic way of referring to science fiction, something started by one of the so-called fathers of science fiction, Hugo Gernsback, back in the twenties. A smerged-together form of "scientific fiction," often shortened to "stf," pronounced "stef" if you valued your life. Or so said those same friends, who had practically had apoplexy when I had been gauche enough to call it "sci-fi."

By the time all that had bobbed to the surface of my mental fishing pond, Mrs. Cartlin was confiding some of her own background to a fascinated Kay.

"Oh yes, I've been reading it ever since—well, not quite since I was a little girl, because Father said girls shouldn't read that sort of thing. But I remember going through a stack of his magazines—*Argosy,* I think—when I wasn't very old. I loved them. Father never did find out, but I was always getting into them when he was away on trips. And I remember when the first issue of *Amazing Stories* appeared. I was married then and bought magazines now and then, whenever I had any money left over from my household allowance. A whole magazine of nothing but scientifiction—I could hardly believe it!"

There was a noise behind us, and I looked around to see Don Thompson standing there.

"The first issue of *Amazing* . . ." His voice was awe-struck and his mouth was practically watering. "I don't suppose you happened to keep any of those early issues?"

Mrs. Cartlin looked at Kay and me questioningly, though she never lost her smile, and Kay hastily introduced Don, explaining that he "collected scientifiction magazines, among other things."

"Oh, how interesting." Even directed at a third party, some of that blue-eyed sincerity slopped over onto me. "You mean those old things would be valuable?"

Don swallowed audibly, and I knew what was going through his mind as he made an attempt to look casual and not overly interested. I'd heard him once, gloating over how he'd found a copy of something called *The Outsider* in a secondhand bookstore and had managed to get it for next to nothing.

"They might be worth a little something to collectors who specialize in that sort of thing," he said. "If they're still in good condition, of course. I wouldn't say they were really . . ."

At that point, the words stuck. His mouth was open to form another word, but nothing was coming out. Then he shut his mouth and blinked. It reminded me of the way Radsack had reacted to her last night, and I wondered if Don would also turn tail.

Kay, I noticed, was watching him closely, waiting to see if anything further resulted from all the abortive motions his lips were making. But nothing did, and she grinned.

"Don't fight it, Don," she said. "You can't win."

His eyes snapped toward her, and his expression cleared for a moment, as if he were relieved to be distracted from Mrs. Cartlin.

"Don't fight what?" he asked defensively. "What are you talking about?"

At the tone in his voice, Kay only grinned more broadly but said nothing.

Again Don swallowed, and his eyes closed for a second. "Well," he said slowly, carefully, "those issues wouldn't be worth much to your average bookstore. But in the right places . . ." He paused again, and then finished in a rush. "They would be worth quite a few dollars."

"My goodness, I never would have imagined. I do wonder if I still have any of them. I remember I threw so much away when I moved into an apartment after Frank—he was my husband —died. I just don't remember. But they might be in one of those trunks down in the basement. It's been so long since I looked . . ."

Kay had pulled a small notebook from her purse and was writing in it. "Here," she said, tearing out a page and handing it across the table to Mrs. Cartlin, "this is the name and address of a dealer. If you do still have any of the magazines, he'll give you a fair price for them."

Mrs. Cartlin took the paper, peered at it a second. "Why, thank you, Miss Clarke. I will look for them, I most certainly will."

"My pleasure, believe me," Kay said. "It's always a kick to find a neo—to find someone who reads scientifiction."

The old woman nodded, still smiling, and put the paper away. "Yes, I know that feeling. I haven't really known very many. I suppose there must be quite a few, or they couldn't afford to publish those magazines, but I sometimes wondered . . . Frank never read a word of it, of course. But, then, he never read anything but his engineering magazines and the newspapers."

She sighed faintly, and again there was a flickering of memory across her face, then a wistful smile. "I never told him about my 'confessions.' I'm sure he wouldn't have known what to make of them. Or of me, either."

"What about the checks you got for them?" Kay wondered.

"Oh, I never showed them to him. I just cashed them. I bought little things for myself or for the house. Or presents for him or the grandchildren." Her smile became amused now. "He used to think it was simply marvelous the way I could manage to pay all the household bills and still have something left over at the end of the month."

Kay and I laughed while Don grinned uncertainly, but Kay made no effort to fill him in about Mrs. Cartlin's salable confessions.

"You know," Kay said into the silence that followed the laughter, "Mrs. Cartlin, you should go to a convention sometime."

"Convention? You mean those political things?" She shook her head firmly. "I was never much interested in politics. Father always said it wasn't suitable—although I have always voted, of course."

"No," Kay said, "not that kind of convention. I meant a scientifiction convention."

"Scientifiction convention? Goodness, what sort of convention would that be?"

"A lot of people who read it get together to talk about it, to listen to authors and artists and each other. There are dozens of them each year."

"There are? My goodness, I never suspected! Why, that must be very interesting. I'll have to try to find out more about them when I go home. Do you suppose that dealer could tell me about them?"

"You don't need to wait that long," Kay said, and I realized from the tone of her voice that this was what she had been, for whatever reason, leading up to. "The world convention is in Melbourne starting the day after tomorrow, and as long as you're already in Australia . . ."

"The *world* convention? You mean people from all over the world who read scientifiction? My goodness!" The interest in the old woman's face had given way to excitement, an almost childlike eagerness.

"Why don't you come with us?" Kay asked. "Unless you have to keep to a schedule . . . ?"

"Oh no; no schedule. I'm not on one of those packaged tours. No, not at all." Her eyes went quickly to each of us in turn, searching for I don't know what. She looked slightly apprehensive. "Are you sure it would be all right? I haven't read any scientifiction lately. I probably wouldn't even know who the authors were any more."

"Don't worry about it," Kay said. "You'll be more than welcome. And you remember—oh, Jack Williamson, say? Or Edmond Hamilton?"

Mrs. Cartlin looked positively awe-struck. "You mean *they* might be there? I never thought . . ."

"It's possible," Kay said. "They come to quite a few. It's settled, then?"

Mrs. Cartlin seemed to be thinking about it yet, but from the look in her eyes, there wasn't much doubt what she would decide.

"I'd really planned to visit Ayers Rock next, but . . . I can always do that later. I do still have enough money to last me another two or three weeks, at least. So I don't really see— All right. Melbourne, did you say?"

"That's right," Kay said. "There's a group of us who flew over from the States for it, and we'll all be taking the train tonight for Melbourne. Why don't you come along with us? There'll be a whole passenger coach full of scientifiction fans to talk to, and even a couple of authors."

"Oh, that does sound perfectly lovely," Mrs. Cartlin said, and I couldn't help but notice that she sounded a great deal more excited about the impending convention than she had about the possible invasion of Earth. "What time does the train leave?"

Kay explained the times and arranged a meeting place while we all got up from the table and made our way to the cashier. Mrs. Cartlin said her farewells and hurried out and up the stairs toward the hotel lobby.

She was barely out of sight before Radsack came zipping up from the opposite direction. From the way he eyed the door that had closed behind her, I wondered if he hadn't been lurking outside the other door until she had left. He had the disk in his hand, and he held it out to Kay even before he came to a complete stop. She took it with a frown and immediately dropped it into her purse.

Radsack seemed to be brimming with energy and enthusiasm as he stood there looking at us brightly. "Have you thought any more about capturing one of them?" he asked.

"The Porovians, you mean? Frankly, no," I told him.

"I've thought about it," Kay said, "but I'm not at all sure I'd want to try it, not without a lot of help. Besides, it sounds impossible. If they can appear and disappear at will that way, what's to keep them from vanishing again, even if we *do* get our hands on one of them? Or what if they send re-enforcements? If any of this is really real—"

"*Now* what are you carrying on about?" It was Don, standing slightly apart from the group now that Radsack had appeared. He was looking nervous again and casting sidelong glances at Radsack.

"You missed the disk's press conference last night?" I asked, earning a startled look from Radsack and a puzzled one from Don. Kay was the only one who grinned faintly.

"The what?" Don asked.

"About midnight last night," I explained, "the disk told us what was going on."

I let Kay fill him in with a summary of the disk's oddly worded explanation, warning, and advice. Don was shaking his head when she had finished.

"You're kidding!" was all he said.

"But I thought you'd become a believer yesterday, after you saw Bob actually vanish," Kay said.

Don snorted, still nervous, still casting sideways glances at Radsack a few feet away.

"I may have become a believer in Bob," he said sharply, "but the rest of this— I don't know how they're pulling it off, but *anything* is more likely than that galactic invasion nonsense!"

Radsack started to move toward Don, opening his mouth to speak, but before Radsack could get a word out, Don turned on him, waving a finger in his general direction. "You Aussies are up to something, I can feel it! You just think you can—"

He stopped as Radsack moved a step closer, and his finger faltered to a mid-air halt. Radsack didn't look threatening despite his height, but rather he looked almost desperate. All the enthusiasm he had been radiating a few minutes before had vanished. He looked the way he had in the hallway last night, when he had practically pleaded with me to come up with a reason for everyone's refusing to believe the alien invasion story.

But Don didn't seem to notice this. He backed up another step, glancing nervously at Kay and me.

"Well," he said abruptly, stiffening his back, "whatever the trick is, you can count me out! I'm not falling for it! Now or ever!"

Then he was gone, wheeling about on his heel and practically running out the door and up the stairs toward the lobby.

Radsack stared after him, his mouth open. "I don't understand," he said plaintively, looking at me, then Kay.

"Neither do I," Kay admitted, then turned toward me. "Has he ever been like this before that you know of?"

I shook my head. "Not that I know of, no. I don't see all that much of him back at the paper, but I'd think that if he'd ever gotten this jumpy, someone would've turned him in. It must just be the apes and the disk and all. Maybe he's starting to actually believe in it, and it's driving him bananas."

"I suppose . . ." Kay mused. "But he started getting nervous back at the airport, practically the minute we landed. Besides, are disappearing giants and talking disks any worse than teleportation and invisibility? He didn't act like this when he ran into that stuff last year."

"But he didn't actually run into it himself, remember?" I said. "He was always offstage when anybody did anything really interesting, but this year he's running into it first hand. He's getting everything at once, really. Maybe that *is* enough to crack his shell. I'll tell you, it was almost enough to crack mine last year, and I got initiated relatively gradually."

"Teleportation?" Radsack was staring at me. He looked and sounded even twitchier than Don had a couple of minutes earlier.

"Something like that," I said. "We'll probably never know for sure, though, since he got himself killed."

"Killed? Who got himself killed?" Radsack was developing a new nervous habit, rapidly licking his lips.

"The guy who teleported," Kay explained.

"Now, when you say 'teleporting,'" Radsack said, the words coming reluctantly and shakily, "you mean he—he vanished? Like that little man yesterday?"

"Not quite like that," Kay said. "Bob just vanishes, but he stays in the same place, physically. The other guy actually moved from one place to another. But in the end he got himself killed." Kay paused, for dramatic effect on Radsack, I'm sure. "By a telekineticist," she finished.

Again Radsack blinked and licked his lips, and he seemed to shrink back from two of us. "A telekineticist?"

Kay nodded calmly. She seemed to be enjoying herself now. "An involuntary one, of course. Whenever he got really frightened, he could move things mentally."

"This—this *really* happened?" Radsack's eyes were getting wider by the second.

"You saw Bob vanish, didn't you?"

He nodded uncertainly. "I think so, but . . ."

"Besides, compared to what's going on here, what is so hard to believe about a little simple teleportation? It's pretty mundane compared to alien invasions, which you seem to accept pretty easily."

"Yes, I—I suppose so. But the one who teleported—he was killed, you said? And the one who—the telekineticist? What happened to *him?*"

"Nothing much," Kay said. "His 'power' only works when he's scared to death, so he can't do anything under normal conditions. No one's been taking him seriously. Just like Bob and his disappearing. A few university types looked at them both for a while, but when some magicians 'duplicated the tricks,' they lost interest."

For a moment there was a touch of bitterness in Kay's voice, overriding the enjoyment that had been there before. "'Powers' like that, which only operate when you're scared to death, aren't reliable enough to be demonstrated on command, so nobody believes in them. Or if you *can* duplicate one at will, nobody believes it's real, and the only way you could make use of it would be to go on stage."

"Yes, I— Yes, that's understandable," Radsack said, glancing around nervously and looking at his watch. "I have to be going," he said, and then he went, just as rapidly and nervously as Don had gone a few minutes earlier.

And just as rapidly and nervously as Radsack himself had gone last night.

"Curiouser and curiouser," Kay mused as Radsack moved out of sight up the stairs toward the street. "Would you say that Mr. Radsack was worried about something?"

"Something like an invasion of Earth? That's enough to make anyone nervous if you believe in it—which he certainly seems to do."

Kay shook her head. "But when he's talking about *that,* he's perfectly calm. Ticked off because no one will believe him, maybe, and badly frustrated, but not panicked by any means. No, it's only when we start talking about Adams and his vanishing and kindred things that he really gets nervous."

I couldn't help but agree, since I'd seen the same thing myself, so I agreed. "But where does that leave us?"

"Puzzled, that's where. Why is he panicked by the possibility that ESP exists and not by the possibility that we're going to be enslaved from space the day after tomorrow?"

I shrugged. "He likes to be enslaved? The logical explanation is simple enough. He doesn't really believe we're going to be invaded."

I suppose that thought had been lurking in the back of my mind for a while, but it felt good when it came out. It was just a bit comforting to make note of something indicating the "invasion" was not real.

Kay was nodding thoughtfully. "But he wants *us* to believe it —desperately."

"All practical jokers want the victims to believe their hoaxes."

"You really think it's a hoax, then?"

I shook my head, and I could almost feel the conflicting thoughts rattling around, clanging indiscriminately against each other, doing nothing to arrange themselves in an orderly fashion, doing nothing whatsoever to help me reach a sensible conclusion.

"Then you *don't* think it's a hoax?" Kay persisted when I didn't verbalize my confusion.

"I haven't the foggiest notion what to think," I admitted. "But I suppose you have it all figured out?"

She laughed. "Hardly. I'm probably more confused than you."

"Impossible."

"Don't be so sure," she said. "My trouble, as you may recall from yesterday's discussion, is that, first, I've actually seen the giants and the apes and all, and, second, unlike you, I've also seen the movies and read the books the clichés come from. It's like—well, like this guy with a white beard and a red suit and eight tiny reindeer comes in for a landing about three feet in front of me, and he hops out of the sleigh and says, 'Ho-ho there, I'm your friendly, neighborhood Santa Claus.' There he is, and I just saw the sleigh floating through the air, and the reindeer are licking my nose, but it's still not the easiest thing in the world to believe."

I agreed with her once more. It was, indeed, hard to believe, but what we'd seen was just about as hard to *dis*believe.

"So what *can* we do?" I wondered aloud.

"I'm working on it," Kay said.

"You are?"

She smiled, a trifle smugly. "I invited Mrs. Cartlin along to Melbourne, in case you don't remember."

"So?"

"So, you've already forgotten what you told me? How Radsack ran away from her last night?"

"No, but—"

"And you noticed the way he avoided her this morning? He showed up the instant she left, not a moment before. He's obviously avoiding her."

"I repeat: So? What does this do for us?"

"So, Mrs. Maydene Cartlin is obviously some kind of esper herself, the way everyone bares their souls to her. And don't tell me you didn't feel it! I saw your face! And I heard you chattering away the same way I was! And Don—you saw how he was struggling to keep quiet about the price of those *Amazings*."

I thought about trying to deny it, even to myself, but there was no point. I *had* felt it—a lot. I'd even halfway joked to myself about her "aura." About all I hadn't said to myself was what Kay was saying to me now, in effect: "Hey, Karns, you just stumbled onto another esper!"

Besides, I was getting used to it. I've spent time with Kay twice now, and both times there were espers under every rock. Either they clustered around science fiction fans or Kay and I together merged into some sort of superserendipiter, which I don't suppose is that much harder to believe in than an ordinary, garden-variety serendipiter like myself.

"Okay," I said, finally, "she's a psionic Mary Worth. What are you going to do, chain Radsack to her and ask him questions and give him a heart attack?"

"Something like that," she said, laughing. "I'll manage to get them together somehow. It shouldn't be too hard on a train. Are you volunteering to help?"

"Why not?" my impulsive half said. "I have to go to Melbourne anyway. I was supposed to go to Canberra first, but my itinerary isn't carved in stone." As long as Mike doesn't find out about it, I added to myself.

Besides, I thought, if I didn't go with them, whatever was happening would undoubtedly continue to happen—around me, not around them. And frankly, if I was going to have to face an intergalactic invasion, phony or not, I'd just as soon have a familiar face or two around, even theirs.

"Yes, Artil? What is it now? I thought I told you I didn't want to hear from you again until after the operation."

"I know, sir, but—"

"And if you don't have anything new to say, don't bother to say anything at all. Bondeach will be here any minute, and I'm scheduled to be with him for the rest of the day, so I don't have time for more of your petty objections. And obviously I will not be able to communicate with you at all while Bondeach is on my coattails."

"Yes, sir. But I've found evidence of other powers!"

"In the same human? If he's that powerful—"

"No, sir, not in the same subject. In fact, the humans who have these other powers aren't even here, but—"

"Very well, then. If they aren't here, you don't have to worry about them, now do you? Is that all?"

"But, sir, just the fact that—"

"The only fact you have to worry about Artil, is the fact that everything has been arranged. The Field Analysis Unit has been prepared. Its crew has been prepared. Even Bondeach has been prepared as best we can prepare him. I only hope that the subjects you have selected have also been at least adequately prepared!"

"But—"

"Carry on, Artil. And be sure to have everyone you've had any success at all with there. No better than you've done so far, we can't afford to leave any of them out."

"But— Very well, sir. Just remember that it was you who ordered this. Just remember . . ."

X

"Why Should We Believe a Wishy-washy Disk That Talks Funny?"

After leaving Kay to plot ways of getting Radsack and Mrs. Cartlin together, I spent most of the rest of the day polishing off Sydney, although I don't think I got more than enough for another two or three rather skimpy articles, mostly on parks and museums. For one thing, my mind wasn't really on my work. It's kind of hard to absorb your standard tourist attractions when you're constantly looking over your shoulder and halfway expecting strange creatures to pop out of the air around you. For another, it was becoming clear that August was not the best time of the year to visit Sydney. It was, after all, practically midwinter, and even the comparatively mild kind of winter they have around here is not great beach weather, and Sydney has a lot of beaches. I didn't bother to visit them all, obviously, but I did cruise by a couple long enough to take some artfully dreary pictures of the deserted sands and a few seagulls, just enough to prove I'd been there.

I couldn't help but wonder, though, whose bright idea this particular fact-finding mission had been. I couldn't imagine that anyone who had the power to arrange a trip like this could also have the innate dumbness not to realize that Australia, being in the Southern Hemisphere, is in the middle of winter in August. I couldn't imagine it, but I couldn't totally discount it, either. In a bureaucracy as big as the *Clarion*, right hands very often don't have the faintest idea what left hands—not to mention Southern Hemispheres—are doing. Orders that come down from on high are rarely questioned. "There *must* be a reason, or he wouldn't have ordered it!" is the standard response to anything that looks —and often is—idiotic. "Australia in the off season? Well, yes, it could be very interesting . . ." Looking on the bright side, though, at least I wouldn't die of heat prostration while trekking through the outback to get a look at the world's largest pet rock next week.

Back at the hotel that afternoon, I found that things had changed a bit, maybe for the better, maybe not. A few of the fans had decided not to go on the train after all but to form a "Sydney Safari." There were to be a half dozen cars, driven by Sydney fans, including Radsack, whose idea the whole thing had been. Recalling Radsack's sight-seeing performance the first night, at least Kay and Don and I were suspicious of his motives, Don vehemently and profanely so.

The rationalizations for the safari were that it would be: a) cheaper, b) more fun, and c) "It's not really a convention unless you get lost at least once, and how can you do that on a train?"

I can't say that any of the three made a great deal of sense, but Kay welcomed the change, particularly when she found out that the organizers had worked out a "seating chart" and that she and Adams and Don and I were all assigned to a car driven by Radsack. By the time I'd gotten back from my tourist duties and had been filled in on the day's activities, Kay had already gotten in touch with Mrs. Cartlin and invited her to go with us in "our" car. And Mrs. Cartlin, despite the fact that none of us were Jack Williamson or Edmond Hamilton, had quickly agreed, particularly after Kay had explained to her that Radsack would be driving. If he was going to be in such close proximity to her for such a length of time, he would undoubtedly break down before the trip was over and "get off his chest" whatever his real problem was, after which he would, equally undoubtedly, be much better off. We would, of course, have to spring her on Radsack at the last minute, but I had no doubts about Kay's ability to do almost anything she set her mind to. As for getting Don into the same car with Radsack, Kay seemed to be in favor of that, too, if only because she thought that his twitchy presence would stir things up even more than would our psionic Mary Worth. And Don himself, after being solemnly and exaggeratedly assured that Radsack was terrified of Mrs. Cartlin, was at least promising to think about it. Personally, I would believe it when I saw it. As for Adams, he would go anywhere you pointed him.

Once the arrangements had been made, Kay and Adams and I spent some time over dinner wondering just what we really *should* have been doing. After all, a possible invasion of Earth, never mind the identity or purpose of the invaders, is a potentially serious matter, and none of us seemed to have been giving it any really serious thought. But have you ever stopped to think what you, personally, would do about something like that? I certainly hadn't, but I was a little surprised to find that neither had Kay or Adams. They'd read about it happening hundreds of times but had never gotten around to thinking about it on a serious, personal level. And the longer we talked about it—even Adams got in a few words—the more we realized that there was practically nothing that we or anyone else *could* do, movies and books and TV to the contrary.

We could, of course, get some guns and hope for the best, although the firearm laws of Australia would make even that rather difficult. And even if we could have gotten them, it didn't strike any of us as a very practical idea. In the first place, there's the standard argument that to anyone with the technology to go from star to star, let alone from galaxy to galaxy, and to vanish into wavery air at will, Earth-style guns would be the equivalent of dart guns or maybe peashooters. Just enough to get their attention if we were lucky, just enough to annoy them if we were unlucky. In the second place, none of us were sure we could even shoot another human, let alone someone who might be a representative of a higher—or at least a different—civilization, especially considering the quality of the evidence against them. As Kay said at one point, "Why should we believe a wishy-washy disk that talks funny?"

Another possibility, the one suggested by the disk itself, was that we try to convince someone in authority that we were being invaded. Great. We might have a remote chance *if* we could actually capture one of the aliens, as suggested, which seemed highly unlikely, even if they did really exist. And even then, unless they were silicon-based instead of carbon-based or there was some other equally spectacular and incontrovertible difference, they'd more likely be written off as freaks rather than invaders.

And without one of them to show around, forget it. Remember what happens to people who report UFO's. And remember that at least one of our very own eyewitnesses still refused to believe it himself.

In the end, we decided that the only two things we could do with any degree of success were worry and rationalize, neither of which was overly productive. And, since rationalization was both pleasanter and easier than worrying, that's mostly what we did. After all, the argument went, there have been thousands of UFO sightings over the last thirty or so years, and a lot of people already claim to have been contacted by them for all sorts of reasons, ranging from good-samaritan benevolence to take-over-the-world viciousness, and nothing has come of it so far, so why should our own little contact case, even assuming it was real, be any different? For all we knew, the other contactees, even the ones who claimed to have been spirited away for views of Utopia on Venus and Arcturus and other impossible places, believed their stories just as strongly as we believed ours. More strongly, probably. So about all we could say for sure was that *something* was going on but that we didn't have the faintest idea what it really was, and in any case, there wasn't much we could do about it except maybe keep a sharp eye out and get a decent set of pictures next time—pictures which, of course, would either be too blurry to be recognizable or too clear to be anything but fakes.

All of which led us to the unanimous conclusion that if anyone *really* wanted to invade Earth, they wouldn't have much trouble as long as they didn't get too blatant about it. If they wanted to infiltrate quietly, who would try to stop them? Who would even believe they existed unless they got terribly careless? Like someone once said about vampires, their chief weapon would be the general public's total disbelief in their very existence.

Oh, if they got really gross about it and hung a large saucer over every major population center and commandeered all the radio and TV frequencies, people might start to worry, but even then there would be a lot who would figure it was all part of an ad campaign for *Son of 2001* or something like that. After all, even in the supposedly sophisticated and technologically minded United States, there were a lot of people who didn't believe we ever landed on the moon, even when they saw the live picture on TV. They figured it was all being done on MGM's back lot, so you can imagine how well you would do with live coverage of an invasion from outer space or from another dimension or whatever. Orson Welles to the contrary, there would be little panic in the streets, and most people wouldn't believe anything was really happening until someone burned down their own personal front door. For one thing, the Mars radio invasion was forty years ago, when the reaction to authoritative announcements was "Really? What should I do about it?" rather than the current "Hah! That'll be the day!"

At least this was the sort of meandering course our rationalizations took as we did our best to bolster our manufactured belief that we were, indeed, doing as much as we could possibly do by attaching Mrs. Cartlin to Radsack in hopes of getting a more palatable truth out of him than we had gotten out of the disk last night.

In any event, when we finished both our eating and our rationalizing, there was barely enough time to collect Mrs. Cartlin, check out, and join the stream of fans heading for the hotel garage. Once there, we spotted Radsack towering above the general rabble easily enough, and I was both surprised and relieved to see that he wasn't driving the Holden. Somehow he had acquired a huge box on wheels that Kay said was a Land-Rover, which at least meant that the five or six of us wouldn't be quite as cramped as I'd feared. On the other hand, I wasn't overly encouraged by Kay's explanation of the metal contraption that stretched completely around the front of the hood and looked like a cross between a horizontal roll bar and one of those gadgets used for mounting snowplow blades. It was a 'roo bar, something that was, she said, practically mandatory for any vehicle that strayed beyond the city limits. If you don't have one and you have the bad luck to mix it up with a kangaroo, you may well finish off the kangaroo, but the car will not be in that much better shape.

Don, having put on a casually courageous face since last he had been in Radsack's presence, had joined us on the way from the lobby as if there was nothing at all out of the ordinary about his action, although I did notice that, as we approached Radsack and the Land-Rover, he drew himself up a little straighter and tried to be unobtrusive about the deep breath he drew in and held for a second or two.

Kay and I shared Mrs. Cartlin's luggage, an extra piece for each of us, and she stayed quietly out of sight by a pillar a few yards from the car as the luggage for everyone was stacked in the rear of the Land-Rover behind the second seat. Once all the cars were loaded and ready to pull out, Kay jumped out, insisting she had to go back to the lobby to pick up some unnamed essential for the trip, and by the time she returned, the other cars had left. It was then that Kay produced Mrs. Cartlin from behind her pillar and slid her into the back seat with Don and Adams while Kay herself pounced into the front seat next to me.

Radsack's immediate reaction to the *fait accompli* was about what Kay and I had expected, but after a brief but horrified stare, he seemed to bring himself under firm enough control to ask what was going on.

Kay cheerfully introduced Mrs. Maydene Cartlin to everyone. "I just met her today, and I talked her into coming along with us to the con," she explained. "I was sure nobody would mind if she rode along with us."

Don agreed enthusiastically if a bit malevolently while Adams nodded an indifferent agreement and I said something brilliant like, "Sure, why not?"

Radsack looked from one to the other of us rapidly, suspiciously. Sitting next to him as I was, I could hear his rapid, shallow breathing, and I think I even could see a pulse throbbing at his temple. He was definitely in a state, and I had the feeling that he might explode any second.

"Of course, if you think it's too crowded," Kay said softly, "we could all still catch the train. We have an hour or so, don't we, Don?"

"Sure," he said. "We've got plenty of time."

"Come to think of it," I added truthfully, "it might be more comfortable on the train in any event."

At about that point, Radsack apparently accepted the inevitable. He didn't relax, exactly; it was more like wilting. His breathing slowed, but the pulse was still throbbing away in his temple. He shrugged.

"What's one more among friends?" he asked rhetorically and resignedly as he turned back to the wheel and put the Land-Rover in gear.

"Now, sir, you do understand the risk involved?"

"Risk, Maurtiss? I was under the impression that this was to be a routine operation that I will be observing."

"Of course, sir, of course. But on a world like this, where the unknown seems to lurk around every corner, there is always a danger, particularly in direct contacts with the natives, such as we plan."

"But you have suffered no losses—if I have read the reports correctly."

"No, sir, no losses. We have been very fortunate, but as I have emphasized to you before, there have been some—some difficult moments."

"Maurtiss, do I have to point out to you again that there is no need—indeed no point—in trying to impress me verbally with the hazards of a facility such as yours. I am an inspector. Therefore I inspect."

"Of course, sir, I didn't mean to—"

"I'm sure you didn't, Maurtiss, but you do understand my position? After all, what point would there be in my taking the time to visit your facility—or any facility, for that matter—if I simply relied on the words and impressions of others? If that were all I did, I could save a great deal of time and expense by simply rereading your reports to the Central Office. Which are, I might add, most detailed and comprehensive."

"Thank you, sir. I do try to see that everything that leaves my facility is in good order. And I do understand your position, and I apologize for any—any seeming impropriety on my part. I assure you, my only concern is for your safety."

"And not for your own?"

"I didn't mean—"

"I'm sure. I appreciate your concern, both for my safety and for the success of my mission. Now—are we ready to proceed at last?"

XI

"Hello? Is Anyone There?"

For the first couple of hours, the trip didn't seem to be living up to anyone's expectations except Mrs. Cartlin's. For one thing, she still held with her philosophy that one simply does not come right out and ask someone, "What's your problem?" You give them enough time and they will eventually come out with it. For another, I suspect that after the first minute or two, she forgot all about the fact that Radsack "had a problem." He kept his back toward her at all times, not even glancing into the rearview mirror in her direction, and at first he kept strictly silent, as if afraid to so much as open his mouth.

As for Mrs. Cartlin, she was totally fascinated by this in-depth meeting with other people who actually read scientifiction and knew what she was talking about when she would mention Hawk Carse or any one of a dozen other totally improbable names such as Epaminondas T. Snooks or Festus Pragnell. Frankly, I thought she was making up at least those last two, but Kay assured me otherwise and even named a book by one of them, *Green Men of Greypec*, which somehow sounded like the sort of thing someone named Festus Pragnell would write. Until now, Mrs. Cartlin had been accustomed to meeting only dumdums like myself ("mundanes," Kay called us, for some obscure reason), who would generally nod in deferential agreement with whatever she said without having the faintest idea what she was talking about, and she was thoroughly enjoying the new experience. After a time, even Don and Radsack seemed to relax a bit and join in the discussion. I was the only one who was pretty well left out, and even for me it was something of an education. Not that I couldn't have lived without it, but it wasn't a total loss.

Except when it came to finding out what was bothering Radsack. There, we found out nothing at all, simply because no one got around to asking him anything about it. Since I was sitting between Kay and Radsack, I could see from the occasional glances she would give him that she was considering abandoning Mrs. Cartlin's genteel, wait-long-enough-and-it-will-all-come-out philosophy and asking a couple of direct questions. Unfortunately, she never quite got around to it, and about two hours out of Sydney, I began to suspect that maybe it was too late for questions anyway.

That was when Kay, after a puzzled frown, like someone who smells smoke and can't tell where it's coming from, looked down at her purse on the floor under the dashboard. As she reached down and picked it up, Don, who had been expounding length-ily on sf predictions that had not worked out, faltered into silence. Then, though Kay hadn't spoken a word, the eyes of everyone in the car drifted toward her. Everyone except Radsack, who had tensed up again. His eyes remained on the road ahead of us, and his hands shifted and tightened nervously on the wheel.

Kay sat silently for a moment, the purse in her lap, her eyes going sideways toward me for an instant. I gave her a nervously wishy-washy smile while I wondered what sort of cloud had suddenly descended on us all.

But it wasn't a cloud, we all discovered a moment later. It was a glow, a pulsing, disconcertingly familiar glow, and it became ghostishly apparent when Kay unzipped the large central section of her purse and slowly picked out the disk.

An extra shiver went up my spine at the sight. Having this thing glow and talk in the middle of a Sydney street or in a well-lighted hotel was one thing. Having it do *anything* out here in the middle of nowhere was another story entirely. Only Mrs. Cartlin, in the back seat directly behind Kay, seemed fully in possession of her cool. With little hesitation once the pulsing disk was in full view, she leaned forward and reached over Kay's shoulder toward the disk. Kay's eyes widened in surprise, but she released the disk. Radsack made an abortive grab for it, but Mrs.

Cartlin had it in her hands, peering at it closely by the time he made the attempt, and the only result was a swerving of the Land-Rover as his attention was diverted from the road.

"Hello? Is anyone there?" Mrs. Cartlin had the pulsating disk three or four inches from her face, talking into it like a microphone. After a couple of seconds of unresponsive silence, she put it closer and repeated, "Is anyone there?" and added a brisk "Over!" as she gave it a solid rap with her finger.

"I don't think it works that way," Kay said. "According to what it was telling us last night, it glows like this when it's warning us there are aliens in the vicinity."

The car swerved again as Radsack twitched a glance toward Mrs. Cartlin.

"Maybe you'd better pull over for a minute," Kay suggested as the Land-Rover resumed the proper track down the road.

Radsack shook his head vehemently. "No, that would make them—"

It was like the night before. Another freeze-frame as Radsack's mouth stopped in the middle of forming another word and the rest of his body stiffened. We were just entering a gentle curve through some rather barren-looking land, what little we could see of it in the headlights, and for a moment the car continued straight, drifting slowly across the road. I was reaching for the wheel myself when he came out of his brief period of suspended animation and jerked the wheel too far, sending us back across the part of the road we should've been on and onto the shoulder. Another jerk brought us back to the center, and so on for several nervous-making seconds as we were all tossed back and forth against each other.

"Kay's right," I said; "whatever's the matter, we better get off to the side of the road before you put us there permanently."

"No! I can't! They—" Again he cut off the words, this time clamping his jaws shut so hard I could hear his teeth click—just like the night before in front of the elevator.

"Who," asked Kay in her best authoritarian voice, "are *they*?"

Radsack didn't answer, only kept his mouth clamped tightly shut, his eyes fixed doggedly on the road ahead. I began to wish we had gotten around to asking questions earlier, before we were out here on a deserted road that looked—

About then I realized something was wrong with the highway. It didn't look like a highway at all, but more like a secondary road. Two lane, but no dividing line down the middle, patchy-looking blacktop. And, now that I thought of it, we hadn't seen another car for at least five minutes . . .

"*Sir?*"

"*Yes, Maurtiss, what is it?*"

"*I believe that the vehicle on the screen contains the subjects. Perhaps you should move back to the observation area now.*"

"*Perhaps. But I can see perfectly well from here.*"

"*I know, sir, but this is the forward area, where the subjects themselves will be brought in, and I thought—*"

"*You thought what, Maurtiss? I thought I made my objectives quite clear. I inspect! I observe the operation first hand. I do not watch from some out-of-the-way cubbyhole. If I had intended to observe second hand, I could have done better watching your recordings back at the Central Office. They, at least, are three-dimensional, while these screens . . .*"

"*I'm sorry, sir, but I have sent requisitions through channels a number of times, and no one has yet seen fit to—*"

"*I'm sure you have. Judging the validity of such requests, however, is not in my department. Now, how soon will the pickup be made?*"

"*If things go according to schedule, in just a few minutes. We will—*"

"*'If?' Is there any reason why this particular operation should not go according to schedule? Is there something you have been holding back from me, Maurtiss?*"

"*Of course not, sir! I was only—*"

"*Very well. Shall we get on with it then?*"

"*Of course, sir, as soon as the preliminary readings are taken.*"

"*Those are necessary? Even in cases such as this? You did say someone had been observing this particular group at first hand?*"

"*That's right, sir. It's standard procedure. Whenever any evidence concerning any individual natives comes to our attention, we assign an—*"

"*I know the nature of standard procedures, Maurtiss.*"

"*Then you also know that standard procedures call for prelimi-*"

nary readings. Now, if you will excuse me, I really must move back to my own post. You are sure that you will not accompany me?"

"Very sure, Maurtiss. Carry on; I will observe from here."

"As you wish . . ."

XII

"Temporarily Can We Malfunctions Cause"

"Where are we? What happened to the highway?"

Radsack blinked at my question like an owl with a full beard and hypertension. Everyone else looked out the windshield at the obviously secondary quality of the road that the Land-Rover's headlights were still sweeping along.

"Are we lost?" It was Don, his voice a notch higher and several notches angrier than it had been at any time in the last two hours. "What is this, the start of another of your scummy tricks, Radsack? Is that it? Wasn't that phony performance in Sydney enough?"

Radsack said nothing. The way he kept his mouth clamped shut, I was surprised I didn't hear his teeth grinding against each other.

"All right, Irv," Kay said, "It's about time some of the truth started coming out, don't you think?"

Still Radsack maintained his quivering, stony silence, and all the while, Mrs. Cartlin kept peering and poking at the glowing disk in her hands. She was turning it around slowly when, without warning, it started talking again. It was the same voice and the same unpredictable word order that had been coming out of it last night.

"Broken through have the Porovians," it said. "Ship have they brought."

Kay and I, who had gotten used to sorting the words out last night, had no trouble understanding the announcement, and, while I can't speak for Kay, the shiver I had felt earlier, when the disk had first started to glow, returned for an amplified encore. The others, except for Radsack, stared at it in varying degrees of confusion, disbelief, annoyance, and perhaps fear. Even Mrs. Cartlin seemed at a loss for words now that the disk had actually answered her.

Not surprisingly, it was Kay who regained her voice first. After a last, suspicious glance at Radsack, she twisted around in the seat, pressing pleasantly against me as she did, and started talking to the disk. No one, least of all myself, was inclined to dispute her status as spokesperson for our group. Even Don, though he retained the angrily fearful look on his face, didn't interrupt with any derisive remarks about Aussiefandom tricks.

"Ship?" Kay began. "I thought last night you said the Porovians operated through 'other dimensions.' Didn't you?"

There was a brief hesitation, just as there had been last night whenever Kay or anyone else had come up with a question that bothered the disk.

"True that is," it said finally. "In time recent, Porovian control strengthened has. Ship sent through has been."

"But why—"

"More difficult for us has it been made," the disk interrupted. "To break through Porovian energy field most difficult is. Time have we little. Most improbable our physical beings transported be to your world in future. Resistance to Porovians by you must be made. Help little we can."

"But you *can* help? A little?"

"At present moment, yes, until cut off completely we are. Porovian ship approaching is now."

At that, everyone—except Radsack, who continued singlemindedly to guide the Land-Rover along the road—darted quick looks at the darkened countryside. Thin clouds had moved in some time before, leaving only patches of stars here and there overhead.

"You can help us escape the ship?" Kay asked. There was, I noticed, a sound of calculated suspicion in her voice.

"Correct that is. Also perhaps capture of Porovian being possible is."

"That's what you suggested last night. We capture one and take it to our leaders. But if they're as advanced as you say and if they're in a ship, how can we do anything like that?"

"Told you we have. Help you will we, for this moment. Resources strained will be, but only chance it is. Interfere we can at this moment, but in your future, independent you must be."

"What you're saying, then, is that you can, without physically coming through to Earth, help us capture one of these Porovians right out of their ship? Is that it? And then, once we have him in our hands, and you've helped us escape, we're on our own?"

"Truth that is. Limitations regret we do, but further contact impossible is."

"How can you help us?" Kay was sounding more and more like a suspicious cop questioning a gang member who had just decided to turn state's evidence for no good reason.

"On Porovian ship, temporarily can we malfunctions cause, until with Porovian have you escaped."

"So we already have a Porovian in our hands when this scenario starts? How do we get on the ship in the first place?"

"Pick you up they will."

Another shudder made the rounds of the car, this time including Radsack.

"They'll pick us up? Why?"

"From you to obtain detection device. Already more than once have they tried."

"Detection device? This disk we're talking to, you mean?"

"Right you are." I almost laughed at the unexpected and presumably accidental colloquialism, but the disk plowed ahead. "Therefore destroyed device must be."

"Can't we just hide it somewhere?"

"Methods have Porovians to locate device. Impossible hiding would be. Into Porovian hands fall it must not. Too dangerous is it."

"But if they know how to locate it, they must know what it is. Why is it dangerous for them to get it?"

Another pause. "Operation of device know they," the disk resumed. "How to build one, know they not."

"All right," Kay agreed, the rest of us still holding our silence, totally unlike the night before, when the disk had trouble getting a word in edgewise. "So, what do you think we should do? How do we accomplish all this?"

"Simple it is." The voice sounded relieved. "Taken aboard ship will you be. Control over your minds, exerted will be. For short period, malfunction and confusion can we cause. Porovian you take and escape. Malfunction and confusion continue we will for maximum time length possible."

"Just any old Porovian? Or did you have a particular one in mind? A small one, perhaps?"

"Concerned do not be," the disk answered, seemingly unaware of the sarcasm that now tinged Kay's words. "For short period, mind control can we exert on Porovian of your choice."

"And you will keep them occupied on the ship while we escape? You'll cover us, so to speak?"

"Correct is," the reply came after another brief pause.

"And what if you get cut off before we get completely away? What if they come after us?"

"Risk that is, but fate of planet on success depends."

"And the disk? How do we destroy it? I haven't been able to put a scratch in it myself."

"Signal to destroy send we will."

"And it will self-destruct in five seconds?" The sarcasm in her voice was now more than just a tinge, but the disk didn't seem to notice.

"Destroy self, yes, but time delay included not," it said.

"Then we have to throw it away before you send your signal?"

"Correct is. Instructions understood are?"

"If you mean, do we know what you expect us to try to do, yes. But when do we get rid of the disk?"

"Signal sent will be shortly. Porovian ship approaching closely is. Becoming short is time."

"How far—"

"Device discard. Destruction signal sent is being."

"How far do we have to discard it?" But there was no answer, and a second later, the disk stopped glowing and a tendril of smoke appeared at one edge. Obviously it wasn't talking any more.

As the smoke increased, Kay jerked around and managed to get the window open a couple of inches and tossed the disk into the night. A moment later, not far behind the Land-Rover, there was a small flash, about like a camera flashbulb.

"Well," Kay said, "it was right about one thing. It did self-destruct."

"Or took our picture," I found myself saying for no good reason. Kay, at least, was polite enough to grin.

"I hope nobody's seriously considering trying to do what that thing wanted us to do," Don said, back in full voice after his minutes of silence. He glanced around at the rest of us. "You aren't, are you?"

"What about you?" Kay asked.

"You've got to be kidding!" He threw a malevolent glare at Radsack. "Let's get this crate moving before we *really* get sucked in by this bunch."

"You still think it's a joke?" Kay asked.

"Of course. I don't know how they do any of this stuff, but— Yes, it's a trick of some sort. It has to be!"

"But on the other hand," Kay went on, "if it isn't, and if we *do* get picked up by this 'ship,' whatever it may be—what then?"

"But they told you—" It was Radsack again, finally breaking his silence, sounding as agitated as ever. "They told us what to do. They'll help us!" The agitation had a tinge of pleading to it, too.

"Buy why should we believe them?" Kay asked. "So far we've only heard their side of it. Assuming the whole thing isn't a gag, of course."

"But why *shouldn't* we believe them? I mean, we've seen what they can do!" More agitation and more of a pleading tone, and the car was beginning to drift dangerously.

"Personally," Kay said, "even if we do get picked up, I vote for *talking*, not grabbing. At first, anyway." She looked at the rest of us. Mrs. Cartlin was nodding.

"Yes," the old woman said, "I agree completely. I always did enjoy a good space opera, but I sometimes think they could have avoided a lot of trouble if they had just taken a little time to talk before they started shooting at each other."

"Any objections, then?" Kay asked.

Don shrugged. "It's better than falling for the gag completely," he said irritably.

I nodded, too, and of course Adams didn't object. Only Radsack was badly upset by this turn of events. Although he had been so badly upset for the past several minutes anyway, there was little difference to be seen.

"But don't you see?" Radsack was imploring us as the car continued to move erratically and I kept a cautionary hand poised in the general vicinity of the steering wheel. "This is our only chance! If we don't take it, Earth is lost!"

Now Kay was looking at him steadily, with the same skeptically questioning look that had been on her face while she had been talking to the now defunct disk.

"That reminds me, Irv," she began. "Just before we were interrupted, I was asking you something. You started to mention a mysterious 'they'—a couple of times, in fact. And I was asking you who 'they' were. Well?"

He blinked disbelievingly. "How can you sit around asking questions like that, when everything may depend on what we do in the next few minutes?"

"The next few minutes?"

"Yes, they will—" Another abrupt stop, and this time I did grab the wheel to keep us on the road. I was about to make a grab for the ignition key when something else caught my attention.

The hood of the Land-Rover was glowing, a lovely fluorescent shade of blue. And sometime in the last couple of seconds, the engine had died. The only sounds now were the slap of the tires on the patchy blacktop and the wind as it buffeted past the windows.

The others had spotted the glow by now, and everyone was peering out the windows, looking for the 'ship' which presumably was causing the glowing and had killed the engine.

"There it is!" Kay was leaning forward, looking up through the slightly slanted windshield.

I whacked my head on the top of the dashboard as I twisted around and tried to get past the shift lever and steering wheel so I could see for myself.

Finally, as the Land-Rover coasted to a silent stop in the middle of the road, I managed to get a look. A hundred yards or so above us, seemingly motionless, was a circular blob. The only light was around the perimeter, a faint, bluish glow, not enough to cast a shadow but enough to show that there was indeed something solid inside the glowing perimeter.

And coming down through the air, linking the center of the blob to the hood of the Land-Rover, was a faintly glowing beam, like a bluish flashlight beam shining through a light mist.

Adams, I noticed as I looked away from the glowing hood and blob for a second, was gone. Invisible, I assumed, but at least not forgotten. Don was getting more panicky by the second, as was Radsack, his eyes darting frantically from one to the other of us.

Radsack twisted once at the ignition. The only result was the clinking of the other keys that dangled from the key ring.

Then, without warning, Radsack threw open the door and leaped, sprawling, to the ground. In the light from the fading headlights, I could see there were stands of some unidentifiable trees along both sides of the road, and a little ahead on the right was a clearing. Radsack, after jerkily regaining his balance, ran with long-legged, ungainly strides into the trees at the right of the road. He was out of sight in seconds.

Then we heard a humming sound, almost high enough to be a whine.

The blob, the saucer, the UFO, the whatever, was coming down in the clearing fifty yards ahead. It was, I could see, your standard model UFO, shaped like two soup bowls, one inverted and placed on top of the first. It looked to be about fifty feet across and a dozen feet from top to bottom at the thickest point. As we watched it settle slowly to within a couple of feet of the ground, I think even Don gave up the idea of its being a joke by Aussiefandom or anyone else.

"Maurtiss! Answer me! I know you're listening! I don't care if Bondeach is with you! I must—"

"All right, Artil, all right! I'm listening. What is it? And it had better be good! Bondeach isn't with me, but you know we're in the middle of the operation!"

"I know! That's the trouble. IT'S NOT GOING TO WORK! Do you understand? IT'S NOT GOING TO WORK! You've got to call it off!"

"*At this stage? Impossible! I gave you your chance. Bondeach is watching from the forward area, just the way we planned, and in a few minutes the natives will—*"

"*But the natives* won't! *They're not going to try to capture him!*"

"*What? What happened? Didn't Verrmond get through to them to explain what was supposed to happen?*"

"*Yes, he got through, but they didn't believe him!*"

"*But by now they can see the Analysis Unit. Certainly—*"

"*There's no 'certainly' about it! They're not going to do it! They told me!*"

"*But why? What are they going to do? What can they do?*"

"*The worst possible thing. They're going to try to talk to Bondeach—ask him questions!*"

"*But why? I don't understand—*"

"*Neither do I! But that's what they're going to do. And if I know Bondeach, he'll answer them! And he'll ask them questions! And the next thing you know, he'll be asking us questions —and with that one human aboard, we can't afford that!*"

"*What? Which human?*"

"*The elderly female known as Cartlin. I told you, it's virtually impossible to keep the truth from coming out when she's around. Don't ask me why! All I know is what it feels like when I'm asked a question while she's near me.*"

"*You're still saying she has some kind of power? Is that it?*"

"*Yes, that is what I'm saying! And the other one, the one who disappears—he's there, too! He had already vanished when I left! Can't you understand—*"

"*I don't know what you're up to, Artil, but if I—*"

"*I'm not up to anything! Can't you get it through your— All right. Put it this way: I can't speak for you or the others, but I can speak for myself. If you go through with this, I will tell Bondeach the truth!*"

"*Artil!*"

"*It's not a threat, just a warning. It's what* will *happen. I won't be able to help myself. If you don't—*"

"*All right! I still don't know what your scheme is, Artil, but I can't risk it, whatever it is. I'll try to call it off. If Bondeach will allow it.*"

"That's all I ask."

"Now get back there! If there is any truth at all to what you say, then you had better keep a very close eye on this group!"

"Of course. Although it might be safer—"

"Get back there! I'll talk to you after Bondeach has left!"

XIII

"You Make Me Sound Like the Hero's Dog!"

Mrs. Cartlin breathed a huge sigh of relief a few seconds after Radsack disappeared into the trees. "Thank goodness he left!" she said. "Now perhaps we can all calm down a bit. My goodness, he was making me *so* nervous!"

Don started to protest, but he didn't seem to have his heart in it. He was still watching the saucer in the clearing, shaking his head. I didn't say anything, and Adams remained both invisible and silent.

Kay let out a breath and looked around at our depleted ranks. "Everyone still agrees? We take it slow? Try to talk to them if possible?"

Mrs. Cartlin nodded vigorously, Don uncertainly. I only shrugged, and there was no way of telling what Adams did, if anything.

"While we're waiting," Kay went on, "what about Radsack? My 'dowsing' didn't have to be operating for me to see that he was more upset than any of us, including the invisible man back there."

Don twitched at the mention of Adams, and he edged toward Mrs. Cartlin, away from the empty but depressed section of the seat.

"The question," I said, with not all that much originality, "is 'why?' Why should *he* be so nervous? He was the one who arranged all this. He was the one who dragged us all over Sydney that first night, and . . ."

My voice trailed off as I noticed Kay nodding. Vague ideas began, belatedly, to surface. It was becoming apparent that, whatever was going on, Radsack had to be involved in it. Also, if his reactions were any indication, things were not going quite the way he had expected—or hoped. But what had he expected? Who was he? Who were the Porovians? The Ormazdans? Apparently they were real, whoever they were, if that thing sitting fifty yards away, glowing softly, was any indication. But what were they *really* doing here? And . . .

"In any event," Kay was saying when I came back out of my mini-reverie, "there's not a lot we can do about this except keep our cool and try to see what's happening and try to establish some kind of communication with whoever's on board that thing. Except you, Bob," she added, looking toward the empty portion of the back seat. "Don't get so calm that you reappear. In case the disk was right, maybe you could cause some confusion and malfunctions yourself."

"I'll try," the timidly shaky voice of Bob Adams said, and Don twitched again and scrooched away from the source of the voice.

For a moment I felt a modicum of amazement at the relative calm I was myself maintaining. Considering what was going on, I should by all rights be screaming across the countryside the way Radsack presumably was.

A second later, I almost did bolt from the car. An opening was appearing in the side of the glowing saucer.

"If Klaatu or Gort comes out of that thing . . ." I heard Kay mutter to herself.

But nobody came out.

The opening was about forty-five degrees away from us, so we couldn't see very far inside, and what we could see didn't tell us much. Just a pale, grayish wall, fairly well lighted. For a moment, a shadow appeared. It looked vaguely humanoid, but at that distance, in my state of mind, it was hard to tell, and in a couple of seconds, it was gone.

Then the opening closed. What looked like a sliding door moved quickly across the opening from the left, and the door was gone. If it had been a door. If it hadn't been an eye taking a look at us. If it hadn't been—

Then the whine started up again, and, slowly at first, the saucer rose straight up. The glow around the perimeter pulsed faintly and then became steady. And for the first time, I realized that, sometime in the last half minute or so, the hood of the Land-Rover had stopped glowing.

About the same time, I remembered the camera stuffed in my pocket. I knew I wouldn't get anything worth while, but I had to try. I just wished my mind had come out of hibernation a little earlier, while the thing had still been in camera range.

I slid across the seat under the steering wheel and out the still-open door that Radsack had exited through not long before. Hastily, I snapped a picture, then another, then ran forward, stopped, snapped another. And another.

Then the saucer, which had been only a receding splotch of light for at least the last two pictures was gone, a point of light vanishing through the spotty clouds.

When I got back to the Land-Rover, Don had climbed out, too, and he looked considerably calmer than before. Adams had reappeared and was standing not far from the car, as were both Kay and Mrs. Cartlin.

"All right, I give up," Kay was saying to the world at large. "What was *that* all about?"

Don shook his head. He was definitely feeling more chipper. "It makes as much sense as most UFO sightings. I've never read about one yet that made any sense at all. Why should ours be any different, just because we had a spirit guide there for a minute?"

"You think it was a standard UFO, then?" Kay asked, her eyes still turned upward toward the spot where it had vanished. "Whatever a 'standard UFO' is. Remember, the disk told us this was the first Porovian ship to come through."

"So?" Don snorted. "The disk was lying. I don't care if there really *are* aliens wandering around loose. I still don't believe that 'invade-we-must' idiocy the disk was handing out. Do you?"

"Frankly, no," Kay admitted. "But I'm pretty positive *something* is going on—something beyond the capabilities of your average Aussiefan."

"What time is it?" It was Mrs. Cartlin, who had been listening intently all the while but now was frowning thoughtfully.

Kay glanced toward her, then down at her outsize wristwatch, easily visible in the reflected glow from the headlights. "About nine," she said. "Why? Do you—"

Kay stopped, snapping her fingers. "You were wondering about lost time, right?"

The old woman nodded. "So many of them seem to operate that way. But not this one, apparently."

"Lost time?" I looked at them puzzledly.

"You know," Don put in, making it sound like only a total ignoramus would be uninformed on the subject. "Whenever anyone gets contacted by the 'saucer people,' they lose an hour or two. The saucer comes down, the little creatures come out, take the people inside one way or another, and the next thing they remember, they're back in their car, driving away. Only it's a couple of hours later than it was about two minutes before, when they were taken aboard."

Then I remembered. "Betty and Barney Hill," I said. "That's what happened to them. But they eventually remembered what happened to the missing time. They said they were 'examined,' didn't they?"

"But they only remembered the missing time after they were hypnotized," Kay said. "All they knew before that was that they had lost a couple of hours they couldn't account for. But we haven't lost any time at all, unless this watch . . ." She held it up to her ear. "Nope, still ticking."

"But there've been all kinds," Don said. Then he shook his head disappointedly. "Too bad this bunch chickened out that way. If they'd taken us aboard, now, that might've made a real story. Oh, we might not be able to get the *Clarion* to believe it, but the *Midnight Inquirer*, now . . ."

He looked speculatively toward me. "Still, if those pictures come out halfway decently . . . and there was the disk, and that big guy that disappeared the first night . . ."

Gradually, as he had been talking, his face had been working up from the initial look of disappointment, through the thoughtful look he had thrown at me, until now there was the beginning of enthusiastic avarice.

"Maybe," he mused, sounding as if he were thinking aloud, "we could even get a book out of it. They've made books out of less, that's for sure. And if we could get Von Däniken or one of those guys to do an introduction . . ."

Now Kay was shaking her head. "But, Don, if you don't really believe—"

"Who ever said you had to believe in something to make money from it?" He looked at me again. "I suppose you still can recite every word the disk said last night? And tonight?"

"I could—for a fee," I added, trying not to depart from the mercenary mood Don had established.

He looked taken aback but he recovered quickly. "How about a percentage? After all, I'll be doing most of the work, and—"

Abruptly, Don frowned and darted a look over his shoulder toward the trees by the side of the road. He shrugged and looked back at me. "Like I was saying, all you'd have to do would be talk the stuff into a recorder. I'd do all the actual work."

"I'll think about it," I said. "What about the rest of us?"

Another frown cut off his reply, and again he looked nervously toward the trees. Where Radsack had disappeared, I thought.

"Did you hear something, Don?" Kay asked.

He shook his head. "No, but . . . It's that idiot feeling again!"

"What feeling?" Kay was watching him closely now, the same way she had been watching Radsack while she had been trying to question him.

Don shrugged, not the usual "I don't know" kind of shrug, but the hunched-shoulder, half-shiver kind you give when you're trying to force an unexpected chill away.

"It's nothing," he said, his voice irritable again.

"The same feeling you've had all evening?" Kay asked. "The sort of feeling you have every time you're around Radsack?"

"What's *that* supposed to mean?" Don snapped, defensively. "And speaking of our fabulous Australian native guide, where did *he* get to, anyway?" He looked at the Land-Rover. "He didn't take the keys with him, did he?"

"Maybe we should look for him," Adams suggested quietly.

"No way!" Don leaned hastily into the front seat of the Land-Rover, across the steering wheel. "*He* ran out on *us*, the— Here, the keys are still here, at least. Maybe this heap will start now that the giant glow worm is gone."

He climbed in, settling himself in the driver's seat, only to find that it was still adjusted for the almost-six-and-a-half-foot Radsack and that his own feet missed reaching the pedals by inches.

"Come on, somebody help me with this seat," he demanded. "It's set for that case of bearded acromegaly, and—"

He broke off as the sound of someone—or something— thrashing through the closely spaced trees by the side of the road reached our ears. We all spun around hastily, and a moment later Radsack appeared, loping out of the woods and onto the patched blacktop at his usual gangling pace. He looked tired and haggard, even in the faint glow from the headlights—which, now that I noticed, seemed to be brightening again.

"What rock have *you* been hiding under the last few minutes!" Don snapped, his tone indicating the words were an accusation rather than a question. "Let's get this crate moving again, all right?"

Don hastily climbed out of the front seat and piled into the back as Radsack stumbled to a halt by the hood and leaned against it heavily.

"I—I guess I just panicked," Radsack said, his voice shaking as he looked around at the rest of us. "I'm sorry."

"You have every reason to be, you—" Don began, but Kay cut him off.

"That's all right," she said, "I can't say that I blame you. But Don's right about one thing. We should get moving."

"Moving, yes." Radsack pulled in a deep breath in an effort to calm himself. Then he looked around. "Is everyone here all right?"

"We're all fine!" Don snapped from inside the car. "Now let's get moving!"

"What's the rush?" Mrs. Cartlin asked as we were all climbing in. "Are they coming back?"

"No, they're not coming back," Radsack said. "At least I don't think they are, but—" Still another freeze-frame performance as he cut himself off, and a moment later he shook his head sharply, as if to clear it. Adams and Mrs. Cartlin had joined Don in the back seat now, and Kay had slid in the front next to Radsack. I got in the front next to her and pulled the door shut.

"Incidentally," Kay said, "do you have any idea where we are? In case you haven't noticed, this doesn't look a lot like a highway."

Radsack opened his mouth, apparently to make a nervous retort, but cut himself short. "I—I suppose I took a wrong turn somewhere and got onto a side road."

He twisted the key in the ignition, and the Land-Rover's engine caught instantly. Without waiting for it to warm up, Radsack put the vehicle in gear and began maneuvering jerkily back and forth across the road, trying to get turned around.

"We'd better go back the way we came," he said as he twisted the wheel with more energy than seemed strictly necessary. "We should get back to the highway before long. We couldn't have been on this road very long, or one of us would've noticed."

Then we were moving back down the road, and I saw that Kay had turned her attention to Don again. She was twisted partly around in the seat, watching him as closely as the near darkness would allow.

"Don," she said finally, "this 'feeling' you keep having—have you ever felt anything like it before? Before these last couple of days, I mean?"

Don, who had been staring out the side window at the passing shadows of trees, glanced toward her irritably. "Not that I remember. But I told you, it's nothing. Let's just drop it, all right?"

"What about yesterday," she persisted, "when those Porovians —or apes or whatever—popped up in the hall at the hotel? Was it stronger then?"

"I told you, let's drop it!"

"It *was* stronger then," she said, nodding. "It was, wasn't it?" There was something soothing in her voice, like it had been last year when she had been trying to coax Adams out of one of his fits of invisibility. At least it seemed soothing to me. I'm not sure about Don. He didn't seem to be in a mood to be soothed by anything.

"All right!" he snapped, turning back to the window. "So it was strong then and it's strong now! Does that make you happy?"

"But you were all right as long as Radsack was gone . . ."

The Land-Rover lurched as Radsack jerked around to dart a look at Kay and then at Don, directly behind him, but he said nothing.

"Is that right?" Kay persisted. "The feeling was gone for several minutes, and it started to come back only when Radsack was returning?"

Don nodded reluctantly, still staring steadily out the window. I had the feeling that if it weren't for the psionic Mary Worth's presence, Don would've died before he admitted to anything as imprecise as a "feeling."

Apparently satisfied with the answers she had gotten, Kay turned back to the front, her eyes pausing as they met mine. I still wasn't sure exactly what she was up to, but I certainly recognized the way she was asking questions. It was the same method she had used with me and a couple of others last year when she had been trying to figure out what particular brands of ESP each of us might practice. She pulled in a breath and looked toward Radsack again.

"Irv," she began, and during the long pause following his name, his eyes darted sideways nervously, touching Kay's face and springing back to the road. "Irv, are you human?"

I know it sounds unlikely, but there was, except for the sound of the Land-Rover itself, a sudden and complete silence. Maybe everyone picked that moment to hold his breath, I don't know. As had happened a number of times before, the Land-Rover began to drift out of the proper lane while Radsack's hands clenched unmoving on the steering wheel. Then, abruptly, he jerked the wheel and, after several more uneven adjustments, got us back on an even keel. He still stared straight ahead, though, and his lips were clamped shut, his eyes wide and unblinking.

"Well?" Kay prompted. "Are you?"

In the back seat, Mrs. Cartlin leaned forward. "Yes," she said after another moment of silence, "I would rather like to know, too."

There was a sound that may have started out to be a laugh somewhere deep inside Radsack's skinny frame, but it was closer to a spasmodic cough by the time it made its way through his throat and between his motionless lips.

"What kind of question is that?" His voice was an excellent impression of Don Knotts at his most twitchily nervous.

"Just a question we'd all like answered," Kay said quietly.

"But whatever gave you a wild idea like that? I mean, why should I be—not be human?"

"Don, and his reaction to you, for one thing. He was reasonably calm all the while you were gone, but he started getting jumpy again—not when you came back but just *before* you came back. As you were approaching."

"So?"

"So, I think there's something about you he senses. The same something he sensed about those so-called Porovians yesterday. That's what's been making him so nervous—ever since he first met you at the airport."

"Come on, Kay!" Don protested loudly. The irritation was still strong in his voice, but nervousness was beginning to edge it out. "You make me sound like the hero's dog in a monster movie, where it always gets nervous and starts howling when the monster is about to put in an appearance."

A faint grin pulled at Kay's lips as she glanced briefly toward Don. "I'm glad *you* said it that way, not me. But that *is* the sort of thing I'm talking about. It's like my emotion dowsing, maybe. I don't know how it works or why, or even when it's going to work. It's just a 'feeling' I get sometimes—like your feelings about Radsack and those apes yesterday."

"But that's . . ." Don's voice trailed away as he looked toward Radsack again. He shook his head and scrunched himself further back into the corner of the seat.

"Well, Irv?" Kay prompted again, turning back to Radsack. "How about it? Don't worry about being attacked or anything like that. We're more curious than dangerous. Okay?" Again her voice had taken on a husky, soothing quality. "In any event," she went on, "we can probably settle it one way or the other when we get to Melbourne, whether you answer or not."

"Settle it?" Radsack's voice erupted, high-pitched. "What's that supposed to mean?"

"There are some fans in Melbourne," she said slowly, "and if my memory serves me correctly, one of them is a doctor—with access to X-ray equipment and all sorts of things like that. So unless your friends come back to rescue you . . ." Still, despite the ominous meaning of the words themselves, the voice was still

soothing. Or so it seemed to me, but that might have been because the words weren't being directed at me.

Again there was the well-known pregnant silence, and after
nearly half a minute, it gave birth to a huge exhalation of breath.

"All right," Radsack said, his voice a shaky whisper, "you win."

"But, sir, I don't understand. You said *you had no objection to
canceling this pickup in light of the field co-ordinator's emergency report. And now you—*"

"I know what I said, Maurtiss. And I know what I meant. I
said that I thought it would be best, under the circumstances, if
the pickup was not made as planned. That is to say, by the crew
and Analysis Unit that you had originally planned to use. I said
nothing about not having another unit and another crew make
the pickup instead."

"But why? If the humans are too dangerous for one, they will
be equally dangerous for another, especially one called up on
such short notice."

"But will they? Will they, indeed? I wonder . . ."

"Sir! Are you implying—"

"I am implying nothing, Maurtiss. I am simply doing the job to
which I have been assigned, as I am sure we all are doing. I am
trying to make an objective evaluation of your facility."

"But how can taking a chance with these potentially dangerous subjects aid you in your evaluation? If the field co-ordinator
is of the opinion that the danger is too great to risk at this time,
then what purpose—"

"Let us just say that I would like to see—and hear—for myself.
After all, as I thought I had made abundantly clear before, what
point would there be in my taking the time and expense to visit
your facility if I simply relied on what others told me?"

"I understand of course, sir. That is the very reason we suggested you observe a pickup personally, but in light of the co-
ordinator's warning, I do feel it would be advisable to use a
different subject or subjects. There is no need to endanger—"

"I appreciate your concern, Maurtiss, but I intend to proceed
in the manner I have already stated. Now, need I cite the
specific regulations which give me the authority to act in this
manner? Or . . . ?"

"Very well, but I must state—for the record—that this action is being taken against my advice and that I cannot take responsibility for your safety."

"That is your prerogative, Maurtiss, and the objection is noted. Now, will you contact the other Analysis Unit? Or shall I?"

XIV

"I Don't Think I'm Going to Buy *This* Gag Either!"

Considering Radsack's situation, his reluctance to admit the truth was understandable. I tried to imagine myself on some other planet, alone in a vehicle with five aliens, not at all sure how they felt about me. I very likely would have been beyond reluctance and into catatonia.

"We win?" Kay seemed to be the only one among us whose mouth and brain were still connected to each other. "That means you *are* an extraterrestrial?"

"Yes." The word came grudgingly, but it came. One final show of resistance, and another sigh.

Then Kay let her own breath out in an even huger sigh as she shook her head. "God! I don't know where to start! I've read about things like this, but what do I— Look, just tell us about it. Tell us about those giants and the apes and the Porovians and the disk and the invasion and— Just tell us *what is going on!*"

For the first time since he had come charging out of the trees, Radsack seemed to relax slightly, a trace of amusement crossing his bearded face. A very human expression, what little I could see of it, I thought.

"Those idiots and their invasion!" he muttered aloud, and again I marveled at how human he sounded, at the odd combination of irritation and resignation in the voice. He sounded, I realized, just like one of the *Clarion* reporters a couple of weeks ago. He had been sounding off about the troubles he was having getting reimbursed for some minor expense or other. "Those clowns and their petty cash fund!" he had muttered, and the tone and expression had been much like Radsack's right now.

Except that Radsack wasn't talking about petty cash.

"Then it isn't real?" Kay asked.

He shook his head. "No. There's no invasion, not the way Verrmond told you."

"Verrmond?"

"The voice you talked to through the disk. He was the one who gave it to you in the first place, the 'giant,' you called him."

"Then he isn't dead?" Kay asked. "But from the way he carried on and then vanished, we were supposed to think he was on his way out?"

Radsack nodded. The car was moving more slowly now and more smoothly as well. "You were," he said. "We got the idea from one of your TV shows a few years ago. But I didn't think—"

"*TV show?*" It was an out-of-step chorus by Kay and Don, but only Kay continued. "*The Invaders,* you mean? That pile of—" Now Kay stopped, too, frowning.

"You've been monitoring our radio and TV broadcasts?" Mrs. Cartlin spoke up now, sounding agedly skeptical. "You're telling us that's how you can speak English?"

Radsack looked blank for a moment, as if not sure what the question meant. "Oh no, nothing like that," he said finally. "We've been here since before your TV and radio were invented. We have complete learning tapes of most of your languages."

Again everyone fell silent, and Radsack glanced around for a second, perhaps to see if we were still there. "Is there anything specific you wanted to know?" he asked.

"You're willing to tell us anything we want to know?" Kay asked, sounding skeptical.

"Anything I can. I was ordered to stick with you, and as long as I do that . . ." He shrugged again, glancing at Mrs. Cartlin in the rearview mirror.

"All right," Kay said, and I could hear the eagerness bubbling in her voice, "there's no point in our— All right. Where are you from? Another dimension? Another star system? Certainly not another galaxy?"

"Another star system, a few hundred light-years away, I understand. You'd have to ask one of our scientists just where it is."

A disbelieving noise came from Don's throat. "You mean you don't even know where you're from? I don't think I'm going to buy *this* gag either!"

"Oh, I know where I'm from. I just don't know precisely where I am. I wasn't the pilot, after all."

"But surely—"

"Oh, I have a general idea," Radsack said, relaxing more with each word. "My world is three or four hundred light-years from here, generally toward the galactic center, I think."

"Like your home town, Don," Kay put in. "It's ten or twelve thousand miles northeast of where you are now."

Don frowned defensively. Even now that it was out in the open, Radsack's presence still bothered him.

"But that's different," Don said. "I could find myself on a map, and—"

"So could I," Radsack said, "if I had a map of this part of the galaxy."

"Galaxy . . ." Kay sounded awe-struck again at Radsack's casual use of the word, but a moment later she pulled herself together. To tell the truth, I'm not sure that I could have done the same. In fact, I'm not even sure that words would have come out if I'd opened my mouth.

"All right," she said, superficially businesslike again, "how did that giant—Verrmond, you said?—and the others vanish that way? Matter transmission?"

"Matter trans— Oh no. Nothing like that. Nobody's ever been able to manage that on any large scale. Do you have any idea how much energy you would have to handle if you converted something into energy for transmission? Unbelievable! I think someone once managed a few micrograms—or perhaps it was milligrams, I'm not fully familiar with the experiments myself— but that's about all."

"Then what is it? How do you do it?"

"As I said, I'm not a scientist. But I suppose the closest thing to it in your stories would be a spacewarp. Or a short cut through another dimension. You know, the kind of thing you have in all your space operas to make interstellar travel possible. There are all kinds of short cuts like that, and we just open them up and step through."

"Your spaceships work this way?"

Radsack shook his head. "No. I don't know why, but these short cuts, they tell me, are only good for a few thousand miles, and only when you're close to a planet. Some authorities think it's the planets themselves that cause them, but—"

"Speaking of things popping out of thin air," I interrupted, startled at the sound of my own voice, "I don't suppose you had anything to do with that wombat a few weeks ago?"

"Wombat?" Radsack sounded puzzled. "I'm afraid I don't know what you're talking about." The others, except for Kay, stared at me blankly, too.

"A few months ago, a wombat appeared in the middle of my desk back in the U.S. And it disappeared a few minutes later, picked up by a pair of large, hairy hands, not unlike those on your alleged Porovians."

"Oh." Radsack sighed. "Probably just someone playing games —unless it was the Phenomena Group."

"Games? Like that saucer back there was playing games?" Kay asked. "Or was that something else?"

"I suppose you could call it a game," Radsack said, sighing again.

"What was it after?" Kay rushed on. "Why did it go away? Did you—"

"There's nothing to worry about. They're harmless—for you, at any rate. Anyway, they're gone and they won't be back. I convinced Maurtiss—"

"You're sure about that?" During the last few seconds, Kay had developed a frown, and now she leaned forward to look up through the windshield again.

"Of course I'm sure," Radsack said. "They're probably back at the base by now. They were only—"

He came to an abrupt verbal halt then, as the hood of the Land-Rover took on what was now a disconcertingly familiar glow, and the engine followed him into silence.

"If your friends have really gone back to their base," I heard Kay saying, her voice sounding strangely distant, "it looks like you've got yourself some competition in the saucer business."

"But I don't understand!" Radsack protested, his eyes wide, but somehow his voice didn't sound as urgent as it had earlier.

This time, from the moment the Land-Rover's hood started glowing and the engine went silent, it was different. The first time, I had felt nothing other than the shock and/or surprise that could be considered normal. Or maybe a bit less than normal, come to think of it, since the edge had been taken off by all the inexplicable carryings-on of the last couple of days. I can't say that I'd been expecting a standard UFO to come floating down that first time, but it was not as totally unexpected as it would have been, say, a week earlier, before the giants and silver-suited apes had built me up to it.

And that first time, we had been in full possession of our senses, such as they were. Not for an instant had things started to fade away.

But this time . . .

There was a dreamlike quality to everything, starting with the faint glow that enveloped the hood and spread over the windshield. The only way I can think to describe it, even now, is to say it was vaguely like when you're driving a long way, late at night, and things on the road ahead start looking like—well, like other things, things that obviously can't be there. The lights in a house at the side of the road, for instance, become the eyes of something big and furry that's about to leap out onto the road. That sort of thing.

Now I don't mean to say that things looked like other things, but there was the feeling of unreality that went along with the "waking hallucinations" or whatever they are. The glass in the windshield, for instance, gave the impression of being soft and two feet thick, and my hands felt as though they were in invisible gloves. It was as if I couldn't really touch anything, as if I couldn't move things directly, only by means of powerful little magnets embedded in my hands. Things moved, but I wasn't actually touching them . . .

Which of course is not exactly what it was like, but I can't think of anything I've ever felt that *is* exactly like what I was feeling.

Finally the Land-Rover rolled to a silent stop, and the saucer, looking the same as it had the first time, lowered itself and hovered about a yard above the road in front of us. It was about then that I heard a noise in the back seat. It may have been a scream, but the sounds were just as strange and unreal as everything else, so it was hard to tell. Or to care. In any event, I managed to work up enough interest to look back, and I saw Don, a look of total terror on his face, forcing the door open and scrambling out—and all, it seemed, in slow motion.

And, for whatever reason, it didn't interest me all that much. Don was escaping the UFO. How nice for him.

I noticed vaguely that somewhere in the distance, maybe a half mile away, lights were zipping along the ground, and now that the door of the Land-Rover gaped open in Don's wake, occasional motor traffic sounds drifted in. In the immediate area, though, there was no noticeable activity now that Don was gone. There were open fields on both sides of the road, bordered by wire fences, and if the saucer had come all the way down to touch the road, it would have crushed the fences on both sides.

But it didn't come down all the way. It hovered, just high enough to clear the fences. I remember thinking—whatever part of me that was still thinking at that point, maybe my upstairs observer, who always seemed to be insulated from reality anyway, so maybe he didn't see that much unusual in the situation—I remember thinking that the driver of the saucer was being extra careful because maybe he didn't carry property damage liability coverage. Which made as much sense as thinking that he was concerned about damaging the fence. Concerned about leaving evidence of its presence, maybe, like those "round burned spots" that show up every so often in the aftermath of saucer sightings.

Then the door opened in the saucer, and I was vaguely intrigued by the fact that it really did look like the door and ramp that Gort and Klaatu had come down in *Day the Earth Stood Still*. Except that here you couldn't see the seams in the metal. The ramp sort of flowed down, like well-controlled lava, and stopped when it came within a few inches of the road. And of course there was the faint glow around the whole saucer, although it was pretty well obscured by the Land-Rover's fading and yellowing headlights.

Calmly, dreamily, we waited to see what interesting thing would happen next.

"Maurtiss, I assume you have been watching?"
"Of course, sir."

"*The one that is running away—is that your field co-ordinator?*"

"*No, sir.*"

"*Then how— Is your restrainment generator defective, then?*"

"*I couldn't say, sir. I can only say that my objections to this action are on record. If you insist on continuing—*"

"*Very well, Maurtiss, if that is to be your attitude, there is nothing I can do about it—at the moment. Please keep in mind, however, that my recommendations at the conclusion of this exercise will carry great weight.*"

"*I realize that, sir.*"

"*Good. Good. Now, shall we proceed? I plan to get to the bottom of this, you may rest assured . . .*"

XV

"Take a Deep Breath and Hold Perfectly Still"

For all I could tell, it could have been a half minute or a half hour before something appeared at the door of the saucer. Oddly enough, what appeared was neither Gort nor Klaatu but a pair of silver-suited apes—Porovians?—short sleeves, hairy arms, and all. They looked pretty much the way I remembered them from the hotel corridor, although I don't think these were the same ones. These looked smaller, although that might have been an illusion because here they were out in the open, not in an enclosed area. The heavy, hairy arms, though, were the same, as were the almost human faces, what little I could see. The backlighting they got as they came down the ramp obscured the faces pretty well. Rather larger eyes than ours, it seemed, and their skin was darker than mine, lighter than Kay's.

And none of us in the Land-Rover moved, not even Radsack. Not that it would have done any good, I told myself, despite the evidence of Don's departure. We should do *something*, though, my upstairs observer kept telling me in a lackadaisical sort of way, even if it was no more than wave hello.

But we didn't.

Not that we were perfectly calm, you understand. Inside my own little cushioned mass of isolation was a knot of—well, not quite outright fear, but certainly a butterfly-making apprehension, not to mention simple curiosity. Radsack—or whoever he really was—had admitted he wasn't human and that he was from a vaguely located solar system a few hundred light-years distant. But he hadn't gotten around to telling us why he or any of the others were here. They weren't "invading" us, at least. Or so he had said. Which left what? We were being observed? Contained? Guided? Helped? Recorded for the folks back home? Exploited? Selectively kidnaped? Played with? True, there seemed to have been a touch of amusement in Radsack's words at a couple of points, once he had broken down and decided to tell all, but who was to say that what was funny to an alien from a few hundred light-years away would be equally funny to a human?

All of which goes to show how our minds wandered (were guided?) as we sat there, of our own free will, waiting for something to happen, waiting for the two apes to make their stately way down the ramp to the road and finally to the Land-Rover itself.

It wasn't until the apes were standing one on each side of the car that I noticed that Adams was still in the back seat, still fully visible. I had more or less expected him to disappear again, the same way he had when the saucer had showed up the first time. But he hadn't. Maybe he was calmed by what Radsack had said. Or more likely, whatever it was that was affecting the rest of us —except for Don, apparently—was damping out his ability to vanish. Or suppressing the fear that made him vanish.

All of us, including Radsack, got out and stood silently, as if waiting for instructions. Our two escorts stood just as silently, and their eyes, large horizontal ovals, fastened on each of us for an instant and then moved on.

As they finished their cursory inspection of us, they stood back, out of our way, and we started walking. There was no verbal order, no sound at all: it just seemed like the thing to do. Telepathy? Or some technological gimmick, like the way they killed the engine? The only way they could communicate? Or just a way of impressing the natives?

With Radsack in the lead, followed by Kay, then me and Mrs. Cartlin, and finally Adams, we moved up the ramp. At the head of the ramp, just inside the sloping top of the saucer, was a small featureless room, roughly cubical. An airlock? A holding cell?

I thought about my camera, still in my pocket with a half dozen exposures left. I thought about it, but that was all. I didn't take it out and point it anywhere. Not because I was afraid to, but because it just didn't seem like the thing to do. In the same way that walking up the ramp *had* been the thing to do, taking pictures was *not* the thing to do. "I guess I'll take a little walk around the block before dinner." It was that kind of decision, that kind of urgency.

Then we were inside, in the little gray cube, and our escorts were missing. Whether they were still outside, or maybe had vanished through a wall, I wasn't sure. All I was aware of was that they were no longer with us.

Then the door was closing behind us. I looked around, vaguely interested, and saw the ramp we had just walked up melt and flow uphill and fill the door, transforming itself into just another wall. And somewhere deep inside me, beyond the reach of my nearly comatose upstairs observer, the twinge of apprehension got a small boost and took a step toward fear. Radsack had said that his friends were harmless, but he had also said they had gone away and would not come back. And Radsack himself was as deeply submerged in mental Jell-O as the rest of us.

And the outside world had just vanished behind a magical gray door . . .

Thoughts of Radsack disappeared as I felt a faint tingle spread throughout my entire body, a mild version of the sort of tingle you feel when you suddenly get out of a cramped position and discover that your leg has gone to sleep. Not painful, but unexpected and startling, even to me in my unreal state of mind.

And I couldn't move.

It only lasted a couple of seconds, and I might not even have noticed my sudden immobility except that it caught me in the middle of a blink, with my eyelids just about two-thirds closed. They froze there, and the whole thing lasted just long enough for me to catch onto the fact that the breath I had been drawing in had also stopped, just long enough for me to wonder—but not to decide—whether or not my heart had also frozen in midbeat. And just long enough for me to remember the "examination" the Hills and others were supposed to have undergone, and to wonder if this was the saucer people's magical way of saying, "Take a deep breath and hold perfectly still."

Then there was another tingle, and it was all over. My eyelids flapped shut and back open like a couple of defective window blinds, and the air resumed its interrupted journey into my lungs.

No sooner was I back in working order than one of the walls of the room melted back, just like the ramp/door had done a couple of minutes earlier. Again I wondered if this was the way they did things normally or if it was just another gimmick designed to impress us natives.

Beyond the new door was another featureless room, and I wondered vaguely if Radsack's friends were terribly unimaginative or if they simply didn't want to let the natives—us—see anything worth while. Although what we could have seen that would have done us any good, I couldn't imagine.

Then, as we stood silently, looking idly around, one of the silver-suited apes appeared from somewhere. For all I could tell, he melted in through one of the walls. He wasn't one of the ones I'd seen before, I was sure. He was slightly larger than the others, and the grayish, silvery suit he wore was cut a little differently. The sleeves, for instance, went almost down to his wrists. He held something the size of a TV remote control in one hairy hand. His eyes shrank, although I couldn't see how they managed. It looked like the way the pupils of our own eyes change size in response to light, but it was the whole eye that changed size. Squinting, I wondered? His version of a frown? A smile?

He moved forward, looking us all over, his eyes roaming up and down each of us in turn. He reminded me of a Nazi inquisitor in an old war movie, the slow deliberate way he moved. I felt like asking Radsack if these were, indeed, his friends and/or employers, but I didn't. Once again, it just didn't seem like the thing to do at the moment. Nothing seemed quite like the thing to do. Nothing except standing and waiting.

Then the ape made a small motion with the gadget in his hairy hand, and everything changed.

The feeling of unreality vanished. That furry, comfortable layer of invisible insulation that had separated me from the rest of the world was gone. Suddenly, I was back in full contact with the world around me, if not with reality.

It took me all of a tenth of a second to decide that it was *not* the sort of world I really wanted to be in contact with.

Imagine that you're swimming along comfortably inside a well-insulated wet suit, breathing oxygen from a convenient tank strapped to your back. Then, in a split second, the wet suit and oxygen tank vanish, and you're over your head in icy water with nothing to breathe, and a couple of shapes you thought were harmless seaweeds suddenly look like sharks. Now convert all of that from a physical feeling to a mental sensation, and you've just about got it.

From the gasps of indrawn breath around me, I assumed that the others except maybe Radsack—had made the transition with me.

Then, although I didn't realize or remember it until later, Adams disappeared. He just shimmered for a second and was gone—and forgotten. Literally. And I don't mean that I just forgot that he was with us. I forgot the very fact of his existence. For a moment, after the shimmering was gone, the name "Adams" floated fuzzily in my mind, and I wondered what it meant. Adams? Who or what was an Adams and why should I be wasting time thinking about him/it at a traumatic moment like this?

Then even that was gone, and there were only the four of us— Kay, Mrs. Cartlin, Radsack, and myself. Or should that be three? Radsack, after all . . .

But there was nothing we could do, aside from bashing our- selves against the solid-looking walls like June bugs against a screen, so we didn't do anything. Except for Radsack, who edged away from us slowly.

The eyes of the silver-suited ape followed Radsack, and in their grimness, I could almost see the glint of swastikas. Then the gibberish—harsh, guttural-sounding gibberish—began, and somehow none of us interrupted, not even Kay, although she did make a number of abortive moves in that direction at first.

"Artil? You are Artil, are you not?"

"That's right, Inspector."

"And these—these are the subjects you have been observing?"

"Yes, sir. Except for the one who—who got away."

"Yes, Artil, I noticed that. Perhaps you can explain. Maurtiss seemed at a total loss."

"*Is he here? I understood that—*"

"*Yes, Maurtiss is aboard the unit. But I am asking the questions. For a routine pickup, this has been most unusual, and I greatly desire to understand. Now, the one who got away—how was that possible?*"

"*I don't know, sir.*"

"*But certainly you must have some speculations. These subjects were, after all, your responsibility.*"

"*I know, sir, but his—his escape took me completely by surprise.*"

"*I see. Do things such as this take you by surprise often?*"

"*No, sir. I—I can honestly say, nothing like this has ever happened before.*"

"*I see. Very well. Perhaps we should approach this from a different direction. What are the special powers these natives possess?*"

"*They—they don't all have powers, so far as I know.*"

"*But those that do—what are they?*"

"*The—older female seems to have the ability to—to force those around her to tell the truth. And the—*"

"*Odd. Of all the powers your facility has reported to the Central Office, this particular one has never been mentioned.*"

"*We have never— This is the first example of that particular power, sir.*"

"*I see. And the others? The young female?*"

"*I'm not completely sure, sir. I have been told that she can detect emotions in others.*"

"*That hardly seems unusual. Even I, for example, can detect that you are nervous, Artil.*"

"*I'm sorry, sir, but— She is alleged to be able to detect them at a distance, when she is out of sight and hearing of the sources.*"

"*This is another previously unreported power? Or have I possibly overlooked it in Maurtiss's reports?*"

"*No, sir, this one is also the first of its type that we have—found.*"

"*And the other? The male?*"

"*He has no special power that I know of, sir.*"

"*And the one who escaped?*"

"It's hard to say, sir."

"The one who escaped, Artil!"

"Yes sir. He seemed to react to the presence of—of non-native life forms."

"Like yourself? Like myself?"

"Yes, sir. As I understand it, it is a power that certain lower forms of native life also possess."

"And yet, there has been nothing in your reports about any of these powers. Don't you find it strange, Artil, that now, on the occasion of my visit, you should come across three never-before-detected powers in the natives?"

"As a matter of fact, sir, it is rather strange."

"I'm gratified that you agree. Do you have any possible explanation?"

"No, sir."

"And you are aware that the readings that were taken on these three just now were all completely normal?"

"No, sir, I wasn't. But I—I wouldn't have expected them to be abnormal."

"But according to the reports, you have obtained unusual readings in the past, have you not? Unusual readings that corresponded with the existence of certain powers?"

"That—that is what I have been told, sir."

"I see. But perhaps it is just that these new, unusual abilities do not register? Could that be it, Artil?"

"I—I suppose that is possible, sir. But I— Sir, if I could be excused?"

"Not quite yet, Artil. Before you leave, I would like to speak to the natives.

"But, sir—"

"Is there any reason why I should not speak to them? They seem to be taking the situation rather well. A bit nervous, perhaps, but that is understandable."

"No, sir, no reason, but— No, sir."

XVI

"You're Not a Porovian?"

The gibbering between Radsack and the silver-suited ape went on for several minutes while Kay and Mrs. Cartlin and I stayed in a cluster near one corner of the featureless room. Though I couldn't understand anything that either of them said, it was obvious that Radsack was getting the worst of it. His eyes were downcast most of the time, and even in the alien language, it seemed plain that Radsack spent a lot of time hesitating and stuttering. My only thought was a hope that all this didn't mean that the ape was telling Radsack that they weren't really harmless after all.

Then, in mid-gibber, I felt something on my shoulder. I jerked and maybe I squeaked, too, as I spun around, bumping into something as I did.

Something that wasn't there . . .

Or was something there? There *must be!* I had felt it, and now I was hearing something, but I couldn't make it out. It wasn't that Radsack and his friend were drowning it out, although they were still trying. It was just that—

I shook my head violently. Another trick to impress the natives, no doubt, although I couldn't imagine why they should feel the need to impress us any further.

But there it was again. A whisper, an unintelligible whisper that was coming out of thin air. It seemed to be saying my name, but that was all I could grasp. It was uncanny, not to mention terribly frustrating. I would hear a word, whispered loudly in my ear, and then another, but by the time the second word came around, the first one would be gone, forgotten. It was like trying to read a book you couldn't keep your mind on, only much worse.

I pulled away, still wondering what sort of alien magic was going on, and why.

Then the voice stopped, and all I could remember was that there had been a voice. None of the words, except a vague remembrance of my own name, remained. Which, with my trick memory, was obviously impossible.

But before I had a chance to consider it rationally—assuming that was possible—I realized that the gibberish had stopped. The silver-suited ape had turned from Radsack, who was still looking hangdog, and was peering at our own little group.

"My name is Bondeach," the ape said. "I would like to ask you some questions." The voice was still guttural and Nazi-like, but now it was speaking unaccented English. Unaccented to my ears, anyway, though to an Australian it would have sounded atrocious.

"All right," Kay said, summoning up more courage than I could find at the moment for myself, "provided we can ask *you* a few things, too."

Mrs. Cartlin nodded in vigorous agreement.

The ape—Bondeach—hesitated, glancing at Radsack, who seemed more determined than ever to vanish into the wall he was now standing against.

"Very well. I don't see any reason not to. Do you, Artil?"

Radsack, who was also apparently called Artil by his friends, shook his head but said nothing. I don't know what his expression looked like to Bondeach, but to the humans in the room, he looked miserable. By the time Bondeach turned back to face us, Kay was already halfway through her first question:

"What are you doing here on Earth? You as a group, I mean, not you personally."

"Primarily, we are observers."

"How long have you been here?"

Bondeach hesitated, glancing toward Radsack/Artil, who said, reluctantly and with no trace of his previously thick Australian accent: "There's been a station here for about a hundred Earth years."

"And what—" Kay began, but Bondeach cut her off.

"I have been given to understand that certain extrasensory powers are not all that unusual among humans, power such as telepathy, telekinesis, teleportation. Is that true, to the best of your knowledge?"

Kay frowned. "They probably exist. In fact, I know that a couple of them exist in rather unreliable forms, but I wouldn't call them common."

"And your own power? The ability to detect emotions? Is that a common one?"

"How did you—" Kay glanced at Radsack. "You told him?"

Radsack nodded.

Kay looked back at Bondeach and shrugged. "Not that I know of. And mine doesn't work very often. Why were you trying to convince us we were being invaded by 'Porovians'?"

Before the question was all the way out, Radsack was cringing. Bondeach's eyes shrank, and he looked toward Radsack.

"Perhaps you would like to answer that, Artil?"

I recognized the same symptoms Radsack had displayed in the car. His hands and arms were stiff, and somewhere under the beard, his teeth were probably clenched. When it became apparent that he was going to say nothing without further prodding, Bondeach looked back at us, his eyes still small.

"Explain the question. I am not familiar with any invasion or with any group called—'Porovians,' was it?"

"You're not a Porovian?" Kay asked.

"Decidedly not. Now please explain."

Kay explained. It took several minutes, partly because Kay would stop after every other sentence to ask a question, all of which Bondeach waved away impatiently. By the time she had finished, Bondeach's eyes had resumed their previous size and they were trained directly on Radsack.

"Summon Maurtiss," Bondeach said, still ignoring Kay's continuing questions, and Radsack obediently vanished through the wall. Bondeach turned back to us.

"Most interesting," he said. "If I understand correctly, if you had followed the advice of the—Ormazdans, was it?—you would have attempted to kidnap me?"

"If you were the first Porovian we saw, yes. But look, when are you—"

Without warning, Bondeach staggered forward. The remote-control-sized box clattered to the floor as his hands clutched at the back of his head. As he regained his balance, he erupted with more gibberish, twice as loud and fast as before, and his eyes swept the room.

Again he staggered, backward this time, his hands going to his forehead. This time, he didn't regain his balance but thumped to the floor. I assume the tight-eyed expression on his face was one of confusion or perhaps near unconsciousness. In any event, he didn't start getting up immediately.

Then I heard the voice and, from the way Kay and Mrs. Cartlin looked around, it was obvious that they heard it, too. The only trouble was, like the mysterious whisper a few minutes earlier, I couldn't understand it. Since it was talking loud and fast, I could occasionally keep two words in my mind at the same time, but even that didn't do any good.

And before any of us realized that we should have taken advantage of Bondeach's momentary incapacity to try to find a way out of there or at least to pick up his remote-control box, Radsack reappeared through the wall.

But this time he wasn't alone. He'd brought along a worried-looking, six-fingered giant with a yellow Brillo pad on his head. Maurtiss, I assumed, and the first thing Maurtiss did was snatch up the box Bondeach had dropped.

A fraction of a second later, I didn't really care. The invisible insulation was back.

And Adams reappeared, both in my eyes and in my mind. Oh, that's interesting, I thought as I saw him standing over the fallen Bondeach, one of his own shoes clutched in his hand like a club; he really can wipe himself completely out of your memory if he's scared enough.

How very, very interesting.

Like I said, the insulation was back.

"Artil! What happened here? What are you trying to—"

"I warned you, Maurtiss! I warned you what would happen! Why did you come back? You left once, and—"

"I couldn't help it! Bondeach exercised his authority as a rep-

resentative of the Central Office. But never mind the reasons!
What happened to Bondeach?"

"*It must have been the invisible one, sir. See, he still has the
club in his hand.*"

"*Invisible? He's not invisible! Artil, what—*"

"*I know he's not invisible now! You turned the restrainment
field back on! He's only invisible when he's frightened, and you
know how the field operates.*"

"*Artil, are you trying to tell me—*"

"*I'm telling you the same thing I told you last time and the
time before that!* These are real!"

"*But—*"

"*Maurtiss! Artil! If you two can stop bickering long enough to
help me up . . .*"

"*Of course, sir. Of course. I'm eternally sorry. I don't understand—*"

"*Very well, Maurtiss, you don't understand. That makes at
least two of us. But perhaps Artil can help us to understand?*"

"*Sir, I don't think—*"

"*I am painfully aware of that, Maurtiss. Now please do not interfere. Artil, tell me, what did you mean when you said, 'These
are real'? There is an implication there that I find most disturbing.*"

"*I—I meant that—that the powers these humans possess are—
are real.*"

"*Artil, let me remind you. You said it was difficult not to tell
the truth in the presence of the elderly female human. As you
know, we of the Central Office also have means—dependable
technological means—of getting at the truth. We do not often
make use of them, but they are available to us. Do I make myself clear?*"

"*Artil, I think—*"

"*Maurtiss, stay out of this! Your turn will come! Now, Artil,
the truth? I can not, of course, offer total immunity, but I guarantee that, one way or another, I am going to get to the bottom
of this, and it will be far less pleasant for those who refuse to co-
operate with me.*"

"*Very well, sir. I—I can see now . . . Very well. These particu-*

*lar humans do, apparently, possess special, extrasensory powers,
as I described. But they are the—the first we have ever discovered."*

"And the reports, Artil? The billions of words that have been
sent in to the Central Office?"

"Untrue, sir."

"I gathered that. But why?"

"If I could explain, sir—"

"Maurtiss, I warned you! Continue, Artil."

"Yes, sir. As I understand it, it began when the Central Office
initiated a—a review of all field observation facilities. The budget
was being trimmed, and . . ."

"And your predecessors were afraid their facility would be
closed down, am I correct? And they then invented these
allegedly dangerous native powers—telepathy, teleportation, and
all the rest—solely for the benefit of the Central Office? So that
the facility here would take on such importance that it could not
be phased out? So that it could even be expanded? So that you
could requisition material of all kinds endlessly? Does that about
cover it, Artil?"

"I—I believe so, sir."

"And the thousands of sets of results from your Analysis Units?
Those, too, were untrue? Faked?"

"Oh no, sir. Those were quite real. Our Analysis Units are
quite busy, and there are often anomalous readings. It is only
the—the powers ascribed to the subjects that were untruthful.
Until now, sir. But now—"

"I see. And the endless facsimiles of material allegedly written
by the humans themselves? Those, too, were generated by you?"

"No, sir! Those were—were all produced by the natives."

"And the events described? The inexplicable appearance of
things? The 'powers' displayed by the humans written about?"

"Well, sir, in some cases, we did play a part in some of the
phenomena."

"Some technological augmentation, you might say?"

"Yes, sir, you might say that."

"I see. And now—"

"Sir! Something is—"

"Maurtiss, I have warned you before! I will not tolerate—"

"But, sir, this is different! The—"

"I'm sure it is. Nonetheless—"

"Sir, we are being surrounded! Just look at the screen!"

"Surrounded? What— By whom?"

"Look at the screen, sir! There are humans everywhere!"

"But how—"

"I—I don't know, sir."

"It must be the one who escaped, sir."

"The one who escaped? Artil, are you telling me—"

"I told you, sir, he seemed to have the ability to—to detect us. He must have contacted his friends somehow, and then led them to us. We had better—"

"Maurtiss! Is this another of your tricks? Are you still trying—"

"This is no trick, sir! You can see for yourself—"

"I can see for myself that a group of alleged humans are milling around outside. I'm warning you, Maurtiss, if those are more of your—your 'field co-ordinators' out there—"

"They're humans, sir! And Artil may be right in his guess as to how they located the unit. In any event, I think we should release the subjects and depart."

"Release the subjects? Of course! That would fit your schemes quite well, wouldn't it, Maurtiss? Release the subjects, and they would never be found again, is that right? And I would have no way of determining their true identities. I would have to take your word that what has been happening was the result of their alleged powers rather than something that you— No, Maurtiss, there will be no release of anyone until I have gotten to the bottom of this! And that can best be accomplished back at the base, where we will certainly be free of further interference."

"But, sir, we have never taken humans into the base! You know that is against regulations! They must be released near the area in which they were picked up, and their memories must be—"

"I know the regulations, Maurtiss! I also know that, as a representative of the Central Office, I have the authority to override those regulations if I see fit. Now let us depart. Unless you wish to bring those on board, too."

"No, sir, of course not."

"Then proceed!"

XVII

"Maurtiss, This Is Simply Too Much!"

I watched and listened with interest but no great sense of urgency as Radsack and Bondeach and the Brillo-headed giant, whoever he was, chattered back forth. Adams, I noticed, remained visible. He also put his shoe back on and joined Mrs. Cartlin and Kay and myself across the room from the other three.

As before, Bondeach seemed to be in charge. Both Radsack and the giant, once they had helped Bondeach to his feet, maintained what looked like a worried and submissive attitude. Every so often, Bondeach would glance in our direction before starting a new harangue.

At one point, the giant, who seemed to have been kicked out of the conversation except for occasional interruptions, cocked his huge head to one side as if listening to an unseen voice, which wouldn't have been that surprising. Shortly after that, he started interrupting in earnest, and a few seconds later, one of the walls of the room turned into a picture window or maybe a TV screen. The resolution was so good it was hard to believe it wasn't a direct image, but after a bit, it dawned on my well-insulated mind that the resolution was *too* good to be a direct image, considering it was dark outside.

At long last, I recognized some of the people milling around out there. Standing a dozen yards back from the screen was Rusty, peering thoughtfully in our direction. Not far away was the one called Eric, and behind him I spotted Denny. At one side was the unnamed "Smo-o-o-th" shouter, a bottle in one hand.

And in the middle of the milling group, held by a couple of hefty types I had seen in the room the night the disk had held its first press conference, was Don Thompson. He was the only one in sight who looked upset, and every so often he would twitch and try to jerk free. The others, although there was no sound to go with the picture, seemed to be behaving generally the same way they had when the disk had been telling them about Porovians and invasions. That is to say, lots of talking and laughing and pointing. I wondered idly if they, too, were being insulated from reality the way we were—or if maybe they were permanently insulated from reality.

It was about then that a couple of things happened. First, the room we were in—and the whole saucer, I assume—lurched. At first, it started upward, getting high enough so that the view of the crowd outside was from maybe ten or fifteen feet up instead of from just above eye level, but then it fell back, wobbling a bit as it did.

At about the same time, the insulation around me began to fade. Not abruptly, the way it had before, but very gradually. Slowly, the mild interest I had been feeling for my surroundings and for the aliens and for the cluster of fans outside became more intense, and the velvet-footed butterflies in my stomach began to grow into something else.

The giant had vanished for a short while, but now he was back, and he and Bondeach were chattering frantically at each other. After one particularly violent outburst by Bondeach, a blue glow enveloped the cluster outside.

Their motors were being stopped, I thought, fully expecting all the laughing and chattering to give way immediately to zombie-like stares.

But it didn't. Everyone kept right on as if nothing had happened. The only difference was, everyone had a faint fluorescent tinge, and they all turned their attention to that instead of the saucer that was presumably still hovering or squatting in front of them.

My own insulation was just about gone by then, and I was starting to wonder with increasing panic how to get out of there. Remembering Bondeach's tone of voice and the way he had been looking at us off and on while he and the giant had been having at each other, I was rapidly convincing myself that, regardless of what Radsack/Artil had told us before, his employers/friends meant us no good.

Then I noticed that Adams was gone again, but at least I could still remember him, which meant he wasn't completely panicked, and we would be better off if we could keep him that way. I started to feel around for him, but a moment later I realized that Kay had beaten me to it. She was standing a few feet away, her hands out in the air as if resting on a pair of low shoulders, which they probably were, talking soothingly but rapidly. As she talked, she kept glancing toward Bondeach and the giant and Radsack, probably wondering if they would ever stop bickering and start answering her questions again.

Mrs. Cartlin was looking around the room, blinking and frowning. Apparently we were all being deinsulated, although I didn't recall the giant doing anything with the little box he still held in one hand.

The saucer lurched again, and this time the view on the screen indicated we had dropped another foot or two. The saucer was probably resting solidly on the ground now. Outside, most of the crowd looked around from their own blue glows toward the saucer, and I could see the lip movements of one of the closer, less fully bearded ones. "Hey, that's a neat trick," it looked like he was saying. "I wonder how they managed it." Or maybe it was just something I remembered one of them saying the night before, when they had been busy ridiculing the talking disk.

Then I heard Mrs. Cartlin. "Mr. Radsack! *What* are you people doing?

Bondeach and the giant didn't seem to hear, so engrossed in their own shouting match were they, but Radsack spun around jerkily at the sound of Mrs. Cartlin's voice.

He started to say something in gibberish, then stopped as he looked at the rest of us. "You're not— You're feeling . . . normal?" He managed to get the words out in English, non-Australian English at that.

"I feel reasonably well, young man," Mrs. Cartlin said. "Now what is going on? What are those two arguing about?" She sounded decidedly impatient.

"But the field—" Radsack glanced toward Bondeach and the

giant, still having at each other verbally. "The field is still on!
And those people outside—I don't understand!"

"The field?" This time it was Kay. "You mean that blue glow?
Is that the same thing that's been turning us into zombies in
here?"

"Yes, but it's not working. It's—" Radsack looked at the screen
again, shrinking back as he did. The cluster of fans, still glowing
faintly, were milling in the general direction of the screen.
"They're not being affected at all! And the antigravity—"

"Antigravity?" Kay's eyes widened, and I could see her tuning
out the here and now, about the way she had when Radsack had
started tossing interstellar terms around casually in the car. "Is
that how the ship works?"

Radsack nodded distractedly, his eyes darting from the screen
and the approaching fans to his still-battling superiors. "Yes, but
it's not working! It's— It *can't* malfunction!"

"And the ships you travel in—you *do* travel in ships, don't
you? From solar system to solar system?"

"Yes, more or less, but—"

"How do they— No." Kay hesitated as if uncertain which of
her thousand questions she should ask next. "How many worlds
have you people contacted? How many planets *do* have intelli-
gent life?"

"How should I know?" Radsack was only half listening to her,
keeping much of his nervous attention on the shouting match in
the background.

"But you *must* know. I mean—"

"It's not my department. There are lots of them, that's all I
know."

More and more human, I thought. How many countries are
there on Earth, sir? Quite a few, right? But a specific number?
Hardly. After all, I'm not a specialist in that field.

"All right, then, why haven't you contacted us before this?
Openly!"

And so it went. Bondeach and the giant yelling at each other,
Bondeach sounding more like Erich von Stroheim all the time;
Kay asking the questions she'd wanted a chance to ask most of
her life; Radsack knowing very few of the answers because they
weren't in his department and because he was paying more at-

tention to important matters, like Bondeach and the fans, than he was to Kay.

It was in the middle of this three-way confusion that another "feeling" started creeping up on me. At first I resisted it, figuring it was just the normal queasiness that goes along with unsuccessfully suppressed panic, but gradually it grew, poking at me to get my attention, telling me in vague and disturbing ways that, for whatever reason, we had better all start planning for immediate evacuation . . .

"Sir, I implore you not to—"

"It is beyond my control now, Maurtiss. It is entirely up to you. If you truly wish to prevent disaster, call off your demonstration."

"But I've told you, sir, it's not a demonstration! What can I do to— I admit, we planned a demonstration for your benefit, just as Artil outlined, but this is not it!"

"So you say. Very well, Maurtiss, I am calling your bluff. It's as simple as that. Whether those are indeed natives out there, with whom you have made special arrangements—which, may I remind you, is still another charge that could be lodged against you! Whether they are natives or your own personnel, suitably disguised, they will be fired upon if this demonstration is not stopped."

"But, sir—"

"Give up, Maurtiss. Have the good grace to admit that you have overplayed your hand. You might have been able to convince me of the reality of some special powers. I have to admit that the way you can make the small one disappear is really quite clever, quite beyond my understanding at the moment. I rather doubt that the scientists attached to the Central Office will be as easily baffled, however. Yes, you might have been able to slip that one and perhaps one or two other simple ones past me. But this! Really, Maurtiss, this is too much! It is an insult to my intelligence! First the restrainment field fails, and then the very heart of the unit, the antigravity, fails as well? You expect me to believe that humans are capable of such things?"

"But, sir—"

"No, Maurtiss, this is simply too much! If these people had

such powers, you wouldn't have an Analysis Unit—or anything else!—left on this entire planet!"

"But these are the first—"

"An even greater insult, Maurtiss, to expect me to believe that now, on the convenient occasion of my tour of your facility, such powers should be newly discovered. You must think that we of the Central Office are total incompetents! Just because we do not get into the field as often as we would like does not mean— Just look at your so-called natives! They aren't even putting on a good act! They look as if this were something they saw every day of their lives! No, Maurtiss, I warn you, call it off or they—and then you—will suffer the consequences!"

XVIII

"Don't You Believe *Anything* Is Real?"

I hate to keep carrying on about "feelings" this way—Don's feeling about Radsack and the other aliens; everyone's feelings when they're around Mrs. Cartlin and her "aura"; that feeling I got last year when I was trying to locate Kay after she'd been kidnaped. Every time I turn around, someone is having a feeling of or about something. Like I say, I hate to keep pulling feelings out of the hat, but I'm beginning to think that most so-called extrasensory powers consist of nothing *but* feelings. Which, I suppose, is a good rationalization for why nobody's ever come up with a good scientific study proving beyond a doubt that ESP really exists— or that it really doesn't exist. Feelings aren't scientific.

But they *are* compelling. At least mine was. I ignored it as long as I could, at least until I convinced myself that maybe my "serendipity" worked more than one way. It not only plopped me down in the middle of weird situations, it also told me when it was time to bail out. After all, if it didn't have a safeguard or two, it wouldn't be a very survival-oriented talent.

I finally got Kay's attention. "We'd better get out of here," I said.

"Why? I haven't—"

"He's right," Radsack said abruptly, shaking his head as if coming out of a cacaphonous reverie. "I should have warned you, but—"

"I know," I said. What with Kay's barrage of questions and everything else that was going on, Radsack was lucky to keep track of his own troubles, let alone ours. "Now, how do we get out of here?" The feeling was still growing.

Radsack, still keeping one ear cocked toward Bondeach and the giant, hurried to a nearby wall and made a couple of quick motions. The wall opened, and we were staring out at two dozen noisy, glowing, blue science fiction fans who, at the sight of us in the door at the head of the ramp, became even noisier.

"Hurry," Radsack said, barely audible over the massed voice of the fans. "Get them all away from here while you can!"

Kay was still holding back, despite everything. "Why? What's happening?"

"Bondeach thinks it's all a trick we're pulling on him," Radsack explained, but from Kay's expression, I don't think she could catch more than every other word over the din. "He's called up his own private ship, and he's going to order it to fire on you! Now move! I'll do what I can! I'm sorry I got you into this, but—" He stopped, looked sharply back at Bondeach, and started back into the saucer interior.

Even though Kay hadn't heard half of what Radsack had said, she seemed to have caught some of my own feeling of urgency, and we hurried out and down the ramp, Mrs. Cartlin right along with us. I could only assume the invisible Adams made it as well.

As we tumbled into the midst of the glowing fans, I managed to glance back. Bondeach was still making like a Nazi and Radsack had joined the giant. Both looked as if they were about to give up on words and tackle Bondeach physically.

Then the door was closing—much less smoothly than before, I thought—and we were in the midst of the milling cluster. Despite what we had seen on the screen inside, it was still dark out here except for the glow from the saucer itself, some auto headlights a hundred yards away on the other side of some trees, and a half dozen flashlights.

As always, everyone was talking at once, and from the phrases and sentences I could catch, it was apparent that everyone was really impressed by the beautiful special effects and they wanted Radsack to come out and take a bow and maybe let them know what fabulous new movie it was all a publicity stunt for.

"Yeah, this is too big and elaborate for anyone in fandom to pull off, that's for sure. It's got to be somebody with money. *Real* money!" That was Rusty, and now he leaned conspiratorially toward Kay. "Come on, Kay, you can tell me. Who's really behind it? Maybe we'll even vote them a special, honorary, spur-of-the-moment Hugo."

Kay, though still somewhat under the spell of her partially answered questions, looked irritated. "Just *look* at all this stuff, Rusty. Don't you believe *anything* is real?"

He grinned broadly. "Oh, sure, a few things now and then. But something like this? A flying saucer kidnaping a bunch of science fiction fans on their way to a convention? No, I just get a feeling about things like that, you know what I mean?"

A feeling . . .

Suddenly, two things happened. First, I realized why the "field" and the saucer's antigravity had failed when Rusty and the others had arrived. And second, I noticed another saucer, a miniature one maybe a dozen feet across, hanging about fifty yards in the air.

And Radsack's words as he had shoved us out the door played themselves back; "Bondeach thinks it's all a trick we're pulling on him. He's called in his own private ship, and he's going to order it to fire on you!"

I didn't know what was going on inside the main saucer, whether Radsack and the giant had been able to outtalk or overpower Bondeach or not, but either way, there was another saucer hanging up there, and I didn't feel like taking a chance . . .

"*FIRE!*"

XIX

"They Shoulda' Quit While
They Were Ahead"

"Look," I yelled, grabbing Rusty's arm and pointing, "there's another one!"

As Rusty looked up, one side of the baby saucer started glowing a bit more brightly than the rest. Then Rusty chortled loudly.

"Hey," he called to the others, "the show's not over yet! Look up there!"

Everyone looked, and the half dozen flashlight beams were suddenly centering on the new craft, swamping out its own faint glow. Once again, everyone was talking.

"Wow! A baby UFO!"

"Must be a midget in that one."

"So that's what happened to Ray Palmer!"

"Nah, it's just a fancy balloon, that's all."

"Yeah, the big one down here's a lot better."

"They shoulda' quit while they were ahead."

"I vote we take away that honorary Hugo we just voted them . . ."

"*I said* fire!"

"*We* are firing, sir!"

"Then why—"

"I don't know, sir! I don't— Sir! We're starting to lose power!"

"What? Have these people gotten to you, too?"

"Sir, I— We're falling! I can't control—"

XX

"All I Promise Is a Half-baked Theory"

The baby saucer lurched and slid sideways down through the air.

"See! I told you it was a balloon. Look at the wind take it!"

"I still think it's sort of cute."

"I just hope Irwin Allen doesn't have anything to do with this. It'd be a shame to waste all these beautiful special effects on one of his crumby stories . . ."

"Hey, maybe somebody finally gave Roddenberry a big budget!"

"Don't be silly. That's just a saucer, not the *Enterprise*."

Kay, I noticed, was still looking irritated and was trying futilely to protest the cavalier treatment everyone was giving the saucers. She seemed to have lost whatever portion of urgency she had gotten from me or from Radsack as we had piled out of the saucer. Apparently she thought that, once we were outside, our problems were over.

I managed to get her attention by grabbing her arm and dragging her away from the crowd.

"There are times," she was muttering, "when these people really tick me off! Being skeptical is one thing, but—"

"Don't discourage them," I told her. "The more skeptical they are, the better. Now if you've got any influence with this bunch, let's see what can be done about breaking up this lawn party while we're still able."

She frowned at me. "What are you talking about now? We're out of the saucer and—"

"I'll explain later," I said, trying to sound as firm and in control as I could. "Just take my word for it that we're not out of the woods yet and we had better get as far away as we can while we have the chance."

"But Radsack—"

"Never mind Radsack or Artil or whatever his name really is. Just help me herd this bunch back to the cars, all right?"

I could see the questions building up in her eyes, like water behind an uncertain dam, but then she blinked again, forcing them back, at least for the moment.

"All right," she said, "but you'd better have one whale of an explanation for me when this is all over!"

"All I promise is a half-baked theory," I said. "Now shall we start the cattle drive?"

She sucked in her breath, turned, and led the way into the cluster and, somehow, in a matter of a couple of minutes, she had everyone moving, generally in the right direction. Behind us, the large saucer simply sat glowing quietly, and the baby saucer finally wobbled and thumped to the ground a hundred yards away.

A few minutes later, when we were all about a half mile away, being driven along the secondary road toward the abandoned Land-Rover, both saucers lurched back into the air, hovered unsteadily for a few seconds, and then shot away into the darkness. Most of the cars in the caravan honked noisy farewells and blinked their lights. As for me, I held my breath from the moment they lifted off the ground until it became apparent that they were heading away from us, not toward us, at which point I breathed a huge sigh of relief. Radsack—or something—must have convinced Bondeach not to mess around with us any more.

Then we were at the Land-Rover, and the five of us—Kay, Don, the recently reappeared Bob Adams, Mrs. Cartlin, and myself—were deposited next to it. Once it was established that the machine could indeed be started, the others moved out, and, with me cautiously behind the wheel, struggling with the archaic manual shift, we followed the taillights the rest of the way back to the highway. Once more we were on our way to Melbourne.

Kay and Mrs. Cartlin blunted the edge of their impatient curiosity for the first few minutes by questioning—or badgering—Don about his unseemly departure earlier and his timely arrival with the cavalry outside the saucer.

He had apparently run all the way from the Land-Rover to the highway, a distance of maybe a half mile, and after a few minutes, the carloads of fans had come by. They had stopped for a snack a few miles down the road and had noticed that the Land-Rover was missing, and then had done a little backtracking to see if it had broken down. They had been about to give up and head back toward Melbourne when they had spotted Don lurching along the side of the highway.

What happened after that was a bit unclear. All Don would say, after he quit swearing about all the "sadistic perverts" in the caravan, was that he had "led them to where the saucer had set down." From what I had seen of him in the crowd outside the saucer, being restrained by a couple of the "sadistic perverts," I suspected that they had used him like an unco-operative dowsing rod. Whichever direction made him the most nervous, that was the direction they went, dragging him with them all the way.

Finally, though, when Kay had gotten everything she could from Don, she and Mrs. Cartlin turned on me. I didn't, of course, have a chance, so I told them what Radsack had said about Bondeach and his private ship, and then plowed into the half-baked theory I had promised Kay.

I started out with my "feeling" about how most of the extrasensory powers were nothing *but* feelings. Nobody really disagreed, although Don snorted occasionally.

"So when Rusty said he had a feeling about the saucer being a phony, it just sort of clicked into place," I said.

"What clicked into place?" Kay asked when I hesitated too long.

"Their skepticism," I said, "their refusal to believe in almost everything. You were complaining about it yourself, remember?"

"I remember, but I don't see . . ." Kay's voice trailed off, and I saw the light dawning in her eyes. I nodded agreement.

"A mass mind," she said incredulously, barely holding back a laugh. "A—a mental mob that disbelieves in *everything!* They didn't believe any of it was real—so as long as they were there, it *wasn't* real!"

"Or at least nothing worked," I said.

H

"So *that's* why you pointed out the baby saucer to Rusty, so they could all disbelieve in it, too."

I nodded. "Before it had a chance to shoot at us. If it really was Bondeach's private ship, and if it really was going to shoot at us."

Kay shook her head. "Extrasensory gestalt skepticism! That must be why they were able to take off again once we were all out of range."

"Maybe."

"But if these people *do* have a power like that . . ." Mrs. Cartlin's voice was thoughtful, musing. "If they do have that power, and if we tell them they have it, then they would disbelieve it, and . . ."

"Another sf paradox is born," Kay said. "It's like going back in time and killing your grandparents before your parents were born. Somehow, though, I don't think we'd better tell them about our theory."

I glanced at her questioningly.

"There's a chance," she said, and I couldn't tell if she was joking or not, "just a tiny chance that they would actually believe it. And then . . ."

Whether Kay was joking or not, I couldn't repress a shudder. The power, if such it was, had come in handy this once, but the thought of Rusty and his group wandering around looking purposely for things to disbelieve was more than this or any other world was ready for . . .